Alpha Male

Alpha Male

William Brandt

Victoria University Press

VICTORIA UNIVERSITY PRESS
Victoria University of Wellington
PO Box 600 Wellington
http://www.vup.vuw.ac.nz

ISBN 0 86473 378 X

First published 1999

'His Father's Shoes' previously appeared in *Sport*

Printed by GP Print, Wellington

To my mother and father

I would like to thank all the members of the Victoria University 1998 Creative Writing MA class and particularly Bill Manhire for his inspirational tutoring. Also thanks to my friends and family, and most especially to my wife Cecile for her unwavering support.

Paradise Cove

'Hey! Aren't you Dalton Frame?'

Obviously the guy had a phenomenal memory. Also, even more obviously, he was a loser. It was written all over his fat face. His T-shirt didn't fit him and he had egg stains on his baseball cap. Besides which I was in no mood for it. I'd just been to visit my dad and I had to get home. On the other hand, it was the first time I'd been recognised by anyone, even a loser, for months. Maybe more. Maybe a year. Maybe more than a year. I couldn't remember the last time. It must have been that stewardess on the way to Palmerston North. Stewardesses . . .

Anyway, loser though he was, I didn't feel like I could just chuck it away. Okay, okay, I know that sounds pathetic, hanging onto the past, hoping to be recognised by a fat-face loser with a dysfunctional forgettory, but that's what fame does for you, as it slips away. And yes, I know it's not his fault he had a fat face. It's not my fault I'm Dalton Frame.

'Yeah, that's right.' I smiled. I was civil. I have always made a point of being civil with members of the public. I wondered what I was going to have to sign. Just hoped it wasn't his stomach. He stepped close to me. Way too close. He was so happy it was humbling.

'Good to meet ya, man.' He shuffled his feet. 'Hey, I was sort of wondering, how would I, you know, how do you get to be on TV? I reckon I'd be quite interested, eh.' For a guy like this, step one would have to be reincarnation on a higher karmic plane, with cheek bones. But I wasn't going to say that.

'Get an agent.'

'Oh yeah, right, and how would I go about . . .'

I smiled again. 'Excuse me.' I got into the car. Fat-face gave me the thumbs up, grinned happily and wandered off. I felt kind of sorry for him, seeing me get into this car. It would only encourage him, poor deluded bastard. He probably thought a red Mark II was standard equipment for actors. In actual fact it was my dad's car, but he wasn't going to be driving it, and my mother hated it, so what the hell. It's an ill wind. I probably shouldn't have said that. Look, I was driving it, okay?

Jamie was trying to stuff his Power Ranger down the demister vents.

'Who was that man?'

'Nobody.'

'Why did he say something to you?'

'Because he was nobody.'

'What did the man say?'

'He asked me who I was.'

'What did you say to the man?'

'I told him who I was.'

'No you didn't.'

'Yes I did.'

'No you didn't.' (Giggles.)

'Okay, smart guy, if you know what he said, why are you asking me?'

'Banana face dumb cluck!' Jamie was at the age where he was aware of humour as a concept but his hands-on experience was limited.

Someone tapped on the window. Not another one, I thought, hopefully. But it was worse than that. I knew her. I knew her, but I couldn't remember her name. Just couldn't get that name. She looked great, too. Her hair was different. How can you know someone's hair is different but not remember their name? She bent down so she was looking at us through the passenger window. It's so easy to tell if a woman's biological clock has started ticking. If they look at you, it hasn't. If they look at your kid, it has. She was looking at Jamie. Such a sweet expression, melting. If she only knew.

'Jamie, roll the window down.' Jamie ignored me completely. He scowled through the window at whoever she was, and showed his teeth. 'Jamie. Roll the window down.'

'No.'

I leaned over and rolled the window down. Jamie bit my arm. He sank his teeth in and hung on. I pretended it wasn't happening. Which, by the way, never works. Because if something is happening it's happening.

'Dalton! Hi! How are you?'

'Great, great . . . you look great.'

'Thanks.' She flicked her hair and prised her eyes off Jamie long enough to glance in my direction. 'It's been ages.' She looked at me like that was my fault or something. The name was close, very close.

'You've changed your hair.'

'Well it has been seven years.'

'Seven years? My God!' The name, the name, I could feel it. She leaned in closer, trying to get eye contact with Jamie. He growled. She had a couple of very fine lines around her eyes. The perfume, that perfume. I remembered the perfume, for God's sake, but the name. Any moment now. I could remember all sorts of other things about her, it was all coming back. She used to tease me. Something to do with gaffer tape. Oh-oh. I could remember kissing her at a wrap party. Or did she kiss me? Or was that someone else who looked like her? Or who didn't look like her? The hair. I could remember hair. Lots of hair. But she'd changed her hair. Was the hair I could remember like her hair now or her hair then? Sally! Her name was Sally. I was sure of it. Jamie stopped biting my arm.

'What's her name?'

'Jamie, that's no way to talk. Introduce yourself properly.'

'Hello, Jamie. I'm Susan.' She wanted to eat him. I could tell, it was written all over her face. Jamie barked savagely and went back to my arm. She wiped a speck of saliva off her nose.

'Is he yours?'

'Yep.'

'How old are you, Jamie?'

'He's five.'

'He's gorgeous.' It must be said, I do have beautiful kids. Evil takes many forms. 'He's so cute. I heard you had a kid, but . . .'

'Two.' I twiddled two fingers and did my impish grin, the one with the dimples.

'Two? You've got two kids?' She laughed. I laughed. She shook her head in disbelief, I nodded vigorously like a village idiot. Jamie lifted his head, snarled and sank his teeth back into my arm. Susan gained control of herself. 'You, of all people . . .'

'Yeah, me, of all people.' Why do people always say that to me? I mean what is so hard to understand about me having kids?

'I can't believe it.' She started to laugh again. 'How old is the other one?'

'Three. She's a girl.'

'Freak out. And you're still with Sam?'

'Uh-huh.'

'Say hello from me.'

'You bet.' Not bloody likely.

And now comes THE QUESTION. '. . . so, are you working?'

'Yeah, yeah, you know, bits and pieces.' The trick being that 'bits and pieces' has to sound like casual understatement as opposed to euphemism. I hadn't worked in twelve months except for a day on a children's show where I had to hold a leech up to the light and laugh maniacally. It wasn't even a real leech, it was just a big slug. They'd flown it all the way from Sydney. It died half way through the tenth take. The director hated me. She kept trying to show me how to look maniacal. She'd shove her face at me and say, 'Like this', doing this incredibly stupid expression. I would then reproduce her expression exactly—I have a gift for mimicry—and she would shake her head and look pained. I found out later I only got the job because the guy they originally cast broke his leg. That was about six months ago, and eight months before that I'd had a day on *American Goth*. I was in a prehistoric bar, dressed in a bear skin. I had to wave my stone sword, scream 'death to the oppressors' and charge at a guy in a tin foil jump suit with a helmet and a six-foot cattle prod. The guy would then electrocute me and I had to fall to the ground frothing at the mouth and convulsing, then die. This director kept getting pissed off because my head was landing in the wrong place. He wanted me to land face down in the puddle of spilt beer. I couldn't walk for two days after that one.

I did, however, have a foolproof way of shutting up people who asked THE QUESTION. I narrowed my eyes and looked deep. 'I'm working on a screenplay.'

'A short?'

'Feature.'

'Wow. What's it about?'

'Oh . . . you know, stuff.' This in a 'I don't want to talk about it because it's too deep and meaningful' tone. Then, switching deftly to 'that's enough about me' mode, and a patronising smile, 'Hey, how about you?' I vaguely remembered her as a runner making the usual noises about directing and short films and writing letters to Martin Scorsese. She was probably a bank teller or an air traffic controller by now.

'I'm producing commercials for Whale.' There was a time when I would have felt faintly contemptuous of someone who was producing commercials for Whale.

'Whale? That's great.' She must have been making a bloody fortune. She started looking at me with this far-away expression.

'We must get together. Talk about your screenplay. We're looking at features.'

'Yeah that would be great.'

Jamie released my arm, and rolled his eyes. 'I s'pose you two are falling in love now?'

'Jamie for God's sake.'

Susan laughed, stood up and gave me her card.

Jamie leaned out the window. 'My grandad's dying. He's really sick and he's going to die because his blood doesn't work any more.'

Susan looked at me. What could I say?

'Dalton, I'm so sorry. He's such a wonderful man.' Susan had met my father? She must have read my mind. 'You brought him on set one day. And he tutored my sister at med school. She thought he was really cool. She said half the girls in the class had a crush on him.' Cool? My father? A crush? A crush on my father? Still, it must be said, it kind of runs in the family. I hope that doesn't sound conceited, I don't really mean it that way. It's just a tool of the trade as far as I'm concerned. I mean if an Olympic weightlifter described himself as strong, you wouldn't say he was up himself would you?

'Is he . . . very ill?'

'Yeah, he's pretty sick.' Suddenly I noticed, over Susan's shoulder, that guy again, Fat-face. He was leaning on a lamp-post, watching us. Thought it was Bradford's Hollywood right in front of his eyes. I thought about giving him the fingers but I knew from bitter experience that this was not a good idea.

Susan stepped back. 'Listen, if there's anything I can do, call me. Okay? Anything at all. We'll talk about that screenplay.'

'Done deal.' I started the engine.

* * *

I pulled the Jag into the driveway, spun the wheel, hand over hand, gunned the engine and lurched up the slope. Every time I did this I missed the MR2. With the MR2 it was all fine motor-control. A little blip on the accelerator as you hit the slope, a twist of the wrist to nip through the turn. God I missed that car. Compared to the MR2, driving the Jag was like docking an oil tanker. Still, the Jag had class, I had to admit that, a ton of class. Real leather.

Jamie attached himself to my ankle and I lugged him across to the house. Lizzie was banging saucepans in the hall. She had three saucepans out but she was only banging one. The other two were full of paint. Jamie ran down the hall and hit Lizzie between the eyes with his Power Ranger.

Children change a woman in many extremely unsubtle ways. They rip her genitals. They cover her with flab. They make her tired and irritable, they make her hair fall out, they completely spoil her sense of fun. They do all these things to the father too, but some of us stay ahead of the game for just that little bit longer. Sam was standing with her back to me, in the kitchen, cooking something. Her weight was on one leg and her hip stuck out to one side like a sway-backed cow. She had paint all over her feet, her hair was a mess and her glasses were crooked on her face.

'How was work?' I went over and kissed the top of her head. How many people in your life do you know by smell? I don't mean their perfume. Sam turned round. She looked tired. She looked a mess. Situation normal.

'Work was okay. How was he?'

'Great. Just jim-dandy. Considering they've given him two weeks to live.' Sam hung her head over the cooking pot and at first I thought she'd forgotten what she was cooking, but of course she was crying. 'Hey, careful. You can always add salt at the table but you can't take it away.' Look, it was supposed to be a light-hearted moment. I tried again. 'Hey, it's my dad, not yours.' That didn't work either. I squeezed her shoulders—nope. 'Oh . . . come on.' Surprisingly enough, not even that worked.

I wasn't handling it well, I knew I wasn't handling it well. The kids came over. Jamie sidled up to her, checking her out, like she might be putting it all on. Lizzie stood by herself across the room with her arms at her sides and her little tummy sticking out. I could see her lip starting to go. I picked her up.

'Is Mummy crying?'

'She'll stop in a minute.'

'Is she crying about Grandad?'

'Now that you mention it, that would probably be it, yes.'

'Daddy?'

'Yes, sweetheart?'

'Why aren't you crying about Grandad?'

'I'm letting your mother have a turn. I'll have one later on when you kids are in bed.' Lizzie struggled to be put down. She went over to Sam.

'Mummy?'

'Yes, darling?'

'I will save Grandad. I will get a big long rope and drag him back from sickness.'

Sam slid down the wall to the floor and sobbed. She dissolved. I couldn't remember the last time I'd seen her like this, and in front of the kids too. I admit it, it was a little confronting. I mean I'm not afraid of feelings or anything like that. Really. I guess I was just a little surprised at how much it was affecting Sam. I mean Sam and my dad were close, I'd always known that. Christ, they'd known each other for ten years. I thought of Susan and the med school girls. Susan was right—obviously he had this effect on women. Can you be jealous of your own father? Of course you can, if you want. But who wants that? Nobody wants that. Somebody stop me.

By now, Lizzie was crying too, and Jamie. All three of them were howling. The kitchen floor was getting wet. Now what I should have done at this point was given them all a big hug. I know that. I should have gathered them all in my arms and held them in a great big arms-and-elbows, salt-and-softness family cuddle. Obvious, right? Right. What did I do? I went for a run. For Chrissake, it was my father. This was actually bugging me, I mean what was supposed to happen when her dad died? Same thing again? I went for a run. Running clears the mind. I'd been doing a lot of running.

When I met Sam she was a weather girl. I used to watch her on TV. 'A region of high pressure will be gradually extending across the North Island.' God I loved the way she used to say that. 'High pressure.' The way her lips came together. That lower lip. The first day we met was in the studio. I was between takes, and she was being shown around by one of the producers, who was obviously experiencing some high pressure regions all of his own.

Between takes, for me, was not downtime. There was a Nintendo in the green room and I used to spend every moment I wasn't on set playing 007. I was determined to get to the Aztec level. I was far more concerned with getting to the Aztec level than with any crap that was happening on set. Really. I'd wait impatiently for the takes to finish so I could get back to the Nintendo room. So there I was heading for the Nintendo room. I had two scenes before I was back and no costume change. Suddenly, Samantha steps out of the kitchen with a Styrofoam cup of espresso in her hand. Our eyes met. God those eyes. She was thinking to herself (she later told me), My god it's Dalton Frame, that spunky guy off *Paradise Cove*. I was thinking to myself, Jesus Christ it's that gorgeous weather girl. But I couldn't remember her bloody name. I damn well should have. I mean Christ she had double the nightly audience I had.

'Oh,' she said, 'you're Dalton Frame.' I had to say something, fast. I couldn't think of anything to say. I was badly rocked. I looked at her.

'You are far, far too beautiful to read the weather.' And then I pissed off. Went straight to the green room and played the Aztec level. I wasted those sons of bitches. That was when I truly knew it was going to happen between Sam and me. Sam was the most beautiful woman I'd ever seen. I collected all these songs like the Dr Hook one 'When You're in Love with a Beautiful Woman', or that Joe Cocker one about you being so beautiful to me. I forget. I forget them all now. But I collected a whole lot of them and I used to listen to them when I was driving around at night, in the MR2. I did a lot of driving around at night in that car. God that was a car.

I collected all these songs about being In Love with a Beautiful Woman, because I was, and it felt like I'd joined a club. The Dr Hook song is actually quite good in that respect. I mean it's a crap song but for all of you out there who have never been In Love with a Beautiful Woman—and let me get this straight, I mean in love, as in, In Love. I mean sure everybody loves a beautiful woman but I'm talking actually so you wonder if maybe you'd love her even if she wasn't beautiful, if maybe somehow the love is on the inside. Stop me if you're going to puke.

Anyway, the point is, once you're really In Love with a Beautiful Woman, as the song goes, you're watching your back. Maybe you're even starting to wish she wasn't quite so beautiful because life would be a lot less paranoid. You're waiting for it all to go wrong. In the words of the airline that isn't our national one, you appreciate that she has a choice. I mean sure you've got a choice yourself. In my case I was spoilt for choice (sorry, but I was). But that doesn't help.

By now I had reached the top of Mount Eden. The top of Mount Eden is quite a place. From the top of Mount Eden I could see my entire past. I could see the house I grew up in, I could see my old school. I could see all the routes I used to follow. My friends' houses, everything. Next to my old school is a prison. When I was at school I used to sit on the wall behind the fives courts and look at the prison walls and wonder what it was like in there. Then my dad sent me to boarding school and I found out. From the top of Mount Eden I could also see Auckland Hospital, standing against the harbour. That's where my dad was. So maybe I could see my future too.

There was a guy standing a little way off from me. He was smoking a cigarette. He was going to seed, he was paunchy, he had grey hair. He was a friend of mine.

'Hey, John.'

'Dalton.'

I knew what John was doing up here. His ex-wife lived on our street. She was a friend of Sam's. He had the kids on weekends, and he picked them up at six-thirty. I checked my watch and the time was ten past. He was up here, smoking a cigarette, waiting for it to be six-thirty before he went to get the kids. How's that? Married for ten years now he can't turn up ten minutes early.

'How's tricks, Dalton?'

'Jim-dandy.'

'Working?'

'Too much.'

John and Jeannie used to come round and have dinner and stuff. Sam knew Jeannie from university and John and I went to school together. We used to play Twister, for Chrissake. We were a kind of meta-marriage. An alliance of couples, a foursome. Nothing kinky, we just—stayed in step. They got married, we got married. They bought a house, we bought a house. They had kids, we had kids. Then John had an affair and they split up. Sam still saw Jeannie, but John stopped coming to the house—he didn't fit any more, kind of like a rogue elephant. I'd meet him for a drink every once in a while, but that was about it. It really hurt. Sam and I cried over that one. Okay, okay, Sam cried. I cried on the inside. But John and Jeannie changed the way I saw divorce. Before, I thought it was something stupid that people did to themselves. After, I realised it was something that could happen to anyone, like car crashes and cancer.

John took a drag on his cigarette. He was looking down the hill. He pointed with his cigarette. 'The old school, eh?'

'The old school.'

I started stretching. I realised I had never once asked John how it felt to be divorced. I guess it was one of those things you don't ask about. Come to that, John had never said anything about my dad being sick. Yes, guys are like that. Yes we are. So what?

'Heard about your dad,' said John. Okay, so I was wrong.

Guys aren't like that.

'Oh yeah.'

'Bummer.'

'Yeah, bummer.'

'Bummer all right.' Well, maybe a little bit like that. John flicked his cigarette away, aiming for the old school. I was cold. Time to get running. I stood up.

'John,' I said, 'what's it like being divorced?'

He looked at me. 'Surprisingly viable, Dalton. Surprisingly viable.'

* * *

'How was work?' This is not the sort of question you would normally hear me asking unless I was in deep shit. Especially since I'd already asked it. It is a very crawly kind of question. We were folding washing, the kids were in bed. Silence. 'I saw John up Mount Eden.' More silence. 'He was telling me that divorce isn't so bad.' No, I didn't really say that. Instead, I poured a Glenmorangie and went to the lounge to listen to some music. I used to watch TV, but now I listened to music. I used to watch TV every night. I'd watch *Paradise Cove*, of course, and the sit-coms. Loved those sit-coms. Those Americans. They can really stick it to you. But I stopped watching TV once I wasn't on it any more. I mean think about it. 'I'm on TV.' What does that mean? It means a hell of a lot, that's what it means. If you're on TV you're on TV you're on TV.

I put on Lou Reed, which was also my little way of saying fuck you because Sam has never been a fan and generally I would desist from playing Lou Reed unless she was out of the house. I put on *Rock and Roll Animal*.

I was thinking about Susan and the med school girls, and John standing there on top of Mount Eden waiting to pick up his kids, and the view of my dad's future.

Lou Reed was singing about heroin. At least my dad would never need to know about the smack. The dope was bad enough. They'd just booted me out of that crap hole of a school for smoking a joint behind the fives courts. He took me into his study and said that to a doctor, which was what he was, using drugs for fun was like spattering solder around a computer to see what would happen. And I said, 'Wow, yeah, I wonder what would happen.' I mean for Chrissake this was a joint. So he said—and this was not the sort of thing he would normally say—'Your mother and I . . . when we make love, we . . . it's very special. Couldn't that be enough for you, Dalton?' He was pleading with me. He was scared and pleading. Now I'm very ashamed about what I said next. I said, 'Man, you want to try sex *and* drugs.'

When I looked up, Sam was standing in the doorway. She said something but I couldn't hear her. I thought, Oh great maybe she wants to make up, so I turned the music off. 'Your agent called.' And she went back to the kitchen. This time I put on *The Blue Mask*. I wasn't worried about my agent. It would only be another audition for a commercial. *The Blue Mask* is one of Lou Reed's many not-so-well-known records. It's about stuff like buying a house and being in love with a woman and doing a few other things you don't normally associate with Lou Reed. Although there are also songs about alcoholism, panic-attacks and self-mutilation (thank goodness). It finishes with a heartfelt love song to his wife. Fancy that.

I took another slug of Glenmorangie. When I looked up Sam was standing in the doorway again. She looked so sorry.

'I'm sorry,' I said.

'I'm sorry too,' she said. She came over and hugged me and that was a very sweet feeling. Salt on her cheeks. It's good that these things stay with us.

* * *

I had been auditioning for at least one commercial a week for the last year and a half. I had got exactly one job, which consisted of an afternoon smiling at a parcel. It's not worth explaining. It does strange things to your mind, that. After the first hour the parcel starts smiling back. When I finished on *Paradise Cove*, I told Charlie, who is my agent, that I didn't want to do commercials. I was an artist. He turned down a large number of lucrative offers. Then the money started to run out and I thought maybe I'd better do a commercial. Just one.

Could I get one? I could get auditions, but I didn't want to audition. I shouldn't have had to audition, Christ, they knew what they were getting, I wanted offers. But after about six months, still no offer, I got worried and I started auditioning. No joy. They'd all moved on. So I started preparing for the auditions. I learnt the lines. I did character work for Chrissake, I'd go to the park looking for a walk to imitate, I'd do animal work, Stanislavski . . . I mean Christ, Stanislavski to sell miracle-scourers? After about six months of this If-I-work-harder-I'll-get-better-and-they'll-give-me-a-job approach, even the auditions were starting to dry up.

Sam went back to work. Back to high pressure and cold fronts. I mean, hey, I'm a modern guy. Seriously. It's fine for Sam to work. If she didn't we'd all be dead by now. And my dad, he bailed us out more than once too. Saved my goddamn life once, but that was nothing to do with money. So, like I say, I'm fine with that. Sam working. But on the other hand, let's face it, it doesn't do a lot for the old mojo. I mean sorry but it just doesn't. So I started running. I'd always been fit of course, but I'm talking about seriously fit. Like, shorten-your-life-span fit.

Anyway, in the end I got an audition, at very short notice, dashed in, didn't learn any lines at all, didn't even know what the part was for. That was the one I got. The parcel job. Nothing since. So in a way that was what finished me with ads. I mean Christ, it wasn't even just that I was bad. At least if I was bad there was a reason. But there was *no reason*. Just no reason at all. There should be reasons for things.

So I rang Charlie the next morning. He was in professional mode, which is always a good sign. If he's friendly and chatty there's nothing going on.

'They want you for Unhip Street Guy.'

'They what?'

'You know the Pepsi ad last week.'

'The Pepsi ad? Last week?'

'They want you. Unhip Street Guy.' It was hard to tell who was the most surprised. Then it clicked. Pepsi, I thought, oh Jesus. Pepsi. American pay scales.

'How much?'

'Before we get onto that, there's a problem.'

'A problem?'

'You'd have to travel. I know your dad's sick . . .'

'Before we get onto that, how much?'

'It's complicated. Four grand to shoot it, guaranteed. But . . .'

'Four grand?!!'

'Wait a second. They're shooting two ads, one in Nepal, one in Queenstown. They'll decide which one they like after they've shot them both. The one they use, they pay more for.'

'Wait, let me get this straight. They are shooting an entire ad, just to see if they like it?'

'Apparently they think they like the idea but they're not sure if it'll work.'

'Which one do they want me for?'

'Queenstown, Dalton. They're going to use Nepalese people in Nepal and New Zealand people in New Zealand.'

'Sounds reasonable.'

'So it's four grand to shoot it. But if they use the ad, there'll be a world buy-out. Cinema, print media, the lot. US TV.'

At this point my heart really began to beat. 'So, I ask you again. How much?'

'I haven't officially spoken money with them, but the indications are, if they use it, we should start at about twenty, twenty-five.'

'Twenty-five? I spent twice that much on my wedding.'

A slight pause, as Charlie didn't say a number of things. 'According to them this part isn't really much more than a featured extra.'

'Extra?'

'*Featured* extra.' The word 'extra' is to me even more like the word 'excrement' than it is to you. Extras queue *after* the crew at lunch-time. They have a different menu. They aren't allowed in the makeup van.

'Well I'm not doing it if they want to treat me like an extra.'

'No, no, no. They won't do that. They know they mustn't do that. She was very complimentary about you.'

'Oh she was, was she? Who?'

'You wouldn't know her. Her name's Susan.'

'Susan at Whale?'

'You do know her?'

'We go way back.'

'Anyway, she says she'd love to use you.'

'As an *extra*?'

Charlie sighed. 'Look, what does Unhip Street Guy do, exactly? What did you do in the audition?' The trouble with Charlie is he's no fun.

'He . . . looks at some girls on the street. Then he follows them up a mountain.'

'Does he say anything to them?'

'Yeah, he says something, of course he says something.'

'What does he say?'

'He says . . . "Hey, hey, hey."'

'Anything else?'

'Not that I'm aware of.'

'All right. Okay. Is he drinking a can of Pepsi?'

'No he is not drinking a can of Pepsi.'

'Who's drinking the can of Pepsi?'

'The girls.'

'The girls are drinking the can of Pepsi . . .' Charlie's breathing got heavier on the line, which always means he's doing mental calculations. He's good, damn good. He's the best damn agent in the country. For a while after *Paradise Cove*, I spent a lot of time worrying that he might fire me. Although technically he would not fire me, he would resign, because it should always be remembered that the actor employs the agent and not vice versa. Charlie finished his calculations. 'There's no way they'll pay more than twenty.'

'For the world? The *world*? The whole of the only known market in the entire universe?'

'They've been crying poor already.'

'Oh please.'

'The market's depressed.'

'The *market's* depressed? How do you think I feel?'

'Well look, Dalton, why don't you just tell me what you want me to do? Shall I tell them to fuck off? More than happy to.' It's moments like these Charlie loves to point out who's hiring who. I told him to get whatever he could, and hung up.

The phone rang. It was Susan. She sounded excited.

'Have you spoken to Charles?'

'Who?'

'Your agent.'

'Oh, yeah.'

'I shouldn't be talking to you, should I?'

'Well . . .'

'But this is social.'

'I guess that's okay then.'

'Well, not entirely social. I just thought I'd suggest, if you are coming down, bring a copy of your screenplay. I told you we're looking for screenplays didn't I?'

'Yeah . . .'

'Wait till you meet the director. Bud is dying to meet you, I've told him all about you. He's such a really great guy, so gifted. And he's looking for a screenplay. I think you two will really hit it off. So . . . you should bring your screenplay. Oh, and by the way do you have a cell phone?'

'Ah . . . it's in for repairs.'

I hung up and I remember I stood for about ten seconds with my hand on the receiver. Ten seconds is not objectively a long time, but if you think about it, it's a very, very long time to be standing in the hall with your hand on the receiver of the telephone you've just hung up. Try it yourself if you don't believe me. It's a significant amount of time, and I took that time because I was dealing with a significant feeling. A feeling that life was changing.

I don't know if you've noticed this, but life changes. It goes along, then it changes. It goes up or down. Then it goes along for a while before it changes again. It might go along for a year, it might go along for five, but the funny thing is that no matter how many times life changes you forget that it's going to change and you think that however it is at the time is how it's always going to be. And then just when it's changing you remember and you think, Oh yeah, life changes. Life changes. It's important to remember that. I was alone in the house. The receiver was cool under my hand. I looked up and down that hallway. That dingy shitty little hallway. I had a job. A dingy shitty little job, but a job. I wanted to tell someone. I wanted to tell my dad. Isn't that something? I wanted to tell my dad. But first I had some shopping to do.

*

It was such a beautiful thing. It was cool and grey and light, and so small. It fit perfectly into my palm. The guy said I could be connected up and talking before I left the shop. I don't know if this ever happens to you but sometimes when someone is selling me something, and the somebody is explaining it in a certain way, how it works or something like that, I go into a trance. I don't know how to describe it. It just happens. The guy said, 'Would you like to see one?' and immediately there was this tingle in the air and my cheeks felt hot.

'Sure.' Trying to sound casual. He reached under the counter and brought it out. It was boxed up. He slit the plastic wrapper with a knife, levered out the staple, opened the box, and pulled the phone out, cocooned in bubble wrap. I was on the edge. The bubble wrap rustled as it came off, and suddenly it was happening. I was in The Zone. Flushes and tingles, skin alive with electricity.

'. . . I think it should be this one here . . .' He was showing me which buttons to push and he had the manual out. Oh God I love it when they have to get the manual out. He turned a page and the paper scraped against the skin of his fingers, sent shivers down my spine. As soon as I was on the street I phoned Charlie and left a message for him to call back.

* * *

They were all standing in the corridor when I arrived. This was not a good sign. The corridor is where they take you for the heavy discussions. They were talking to the registrar. He was this young guy in Armani jeans and a T-shirt under his white coat and he always had a can of Diet Coke in his hand. Every time I ever saw him he always had this can of Diet Coke. He'd been watching too much *E.R.* Everyone was gathered round him. That's to say my mother, my sister and my brother. He was winding up a little speech about pain control.

'The most important thing from here on is pain control. No matter what else, we must be absolutely sure that he is not in pain.' He took a swig of Coke and looked at my mother, like he'd just said something extremely contentious.

My mother looked awful. She looked like a ghost. She looked worse than my father. She was doing it on purpose; the worse she looked the better she felt. My sister looked great. I think with her, the worse she felt the better she looked. My brother looked pissed off, but he always looks like that. I don't know how I looked. I spoke to my brother.

'Did I miss something?'

My brother Jason, who is a foot taller than me, is usually the one who does the talking. My brother has made a fortune selling pharmaceuticals to hospitals, and he is the hairiest guy in the universe. What else can I say about him? He's my brother. My brother opened his mouth, but then he shut it. Immediately I knew something serious was happening. It was my mother who said it.

'If he gets another chest infection, they're not going to use antibiotics.'

'But if they don't use antibiotics . . .'

'I think what the doctor is saying is there's no point in prolonging the inevitable.' This was my brother. E.R. nodded. He approved of my brother.

'From whose point of view?' E.R. looked at his watch. He didn't approve of me.

'I think he wants to go. I think we should tell him it's okay to die. I don't think he knows that yet.' This was my sister. My sister Lynette is the same height as me. No, I'm not short, I'm just not particularly tall. Lynette has made a modest living restoring furniture and I have no idea how hairy she is. My sister looked at my mother. My mother looked at the door to my dad's room, which was just behind us. We all looked at my mother. My mother swayed and my brother caught her.

'So how long has he got?' This was me again. Doctors think this is the most tasteless question you can ask, because they never know the answer.

'It's hard to say,' (swigs on coke). 'But certainly days rather than weeks.' Days, I thought to myself. Days, that's heaps of time. That's forever. It's strange, it was like, as long as it wasn't happening now, it wasn't happening. The less time there was, the more short term the thinking became.

My cell phone rang. I knew who was calling—Charlie was the only one who had the number. 'Hi, Charlie, look I can't talk now I'll call you back.' The greatest pleasure of the cell phone is *not* talking to someone on it. It feels so good to snap that little mouth bit shut again and shove it back in your pocket. My brother was looking at my cell phone.

'Hey. I had to get it. Everyone's got one.'

'Everyone with a job.'

'So, I've got a job. All right?'

E.R. decided he wasn't needed anymore. He took another swig of Coke and sauntered off down the corridor. My sister kissed me on the cheek.

'Well done, Dalton.'

'Why, thank you.' I looked at my brother, like if only he could have been half so gracious. Don't get me wrong. I love the guy. I decided now was as good a time as any to break the news. 'In fact I'm going to have to go away for the weekend. We're shooting in Queenstown.'

'This weekend?' My brother looked more pissed off than ever.

'It's a job.'

'You realise what could happen?'

'Don't be melodramatic.'

'You heard him.' He jerked a thumb down the corridor.

'Look . . .' I wanted to say, Look Jason, if I don't do this job I might as well kiss the whole thing goodbye, but I went all squeaky. My mother, of all people, surprised me. 'Of course you have to go, dear,' she said. 'Life must go on.' And she went through the door. My sister gave me another kiss and followed her. It was just me and my brother. He looked even more pissed off than before.

'Hey, my loss, right?'

'I just thought you'd be here.' He stopped looking pissed off and his face went red.

'Oh shit.'

'Just . . . stay in touch. Okay?'

I patted the cell phone in my pocket. 'What do you think I got this for?'

I rang Charlie back on the way down Broadway, in the Jag. That phone call felt good, I can tell you. I could see a woman in a Saab checking me out at the lights. I was beginning to think maybe I could get used to that Jag. It had a kind of Olde Worlde charm which contrasted nicely with the cell phone. The MR2 wouldn't have had the same effect at all. Use a cell phone in an MR2 and you could be anybody. You could be a plumbing contractor. But a cell phone in a 1961 Mk II, that's something. Charlie sounded pleased.

'They'll pay you five for the weekend but twenty for world is tops.'

'Twenty?'

'I swear, I fought like hell.'

'Twenty . . . Jesus . . .' I was thrilled, of course I was thrilled. But it just felt so great to be bitching and moaning and arguing on a cell phone about thousands of dollars. Thousands of my dollars. I began to wonder if maybe producing might be quite fun. Arguing on a cell phone about millions of other people's dollars. I'd have to ask Susan.

*

Then, more shopping. I had to get to the gym before I picked Jamie up at three, and I still hadn't found the right pair of sunglasses. A pair of sunglasses in the mountains is essential. I had found a pair of Vuarnets which I knew would do the business eye protection-wise but I wasn't so sure on the appearance front. They were good, but were they good enough? The guy in the shop was not good, not good at all, and I was starting to sweat it.

Then, to make matters worse, I turned around and I bumped into Toby. Toby was one of those guys who drive you crazy. He was an actor. He was a short guy, with a broken nose. He specialised in tough bastards. Tough bastard supporting roles, you know, like the guy in the cliff-hanger that looks like he's about to smash your face in next week, or the main crook's sidekick that gets his nuts shot off when he can't find the girl with the heroin in her suitcase except it isn't her suitcase but she picked it up by mistake at the airport. One of those guys.

'Hey, my man!' Toby hugged me. Hugging is something that some guys do. Toby is one of those guys; I am not. I will hug women. Guys, I will not hug. Toby also likes to put his face really close to yours. No he doesn't have bad breath, no he doesn't have enlarged pores. But still.

'I'm good, Toby.' If you really want to know, the thing about Toby that I really hate is he doesn't treat me with respect. He's as friendly as a puppy, but the fact is I have a certain amount of track in my record, and yes it does irritate me when a young guy who is basically a loser, who will never be a leading man, who just does not have the profile for it, who will always be second thug from the right, just climbs right into my face like that. I do not like it. Call me a snob. You're a snob. Okay, I'm a snob. I can't help myself.

'You working?' God THAT QUESTION again. This is exactly the sort of thing I mean. A guy like him just shouldn't be asking that question of a guy like me. Everybody knows that.

'Yes, Toby, I am working. How about you?'

'Six months on *Paradise Cove*.' He shadow-boxes round and round me, jabbing me in the ribs. Oh Jesus. It's like a knife in the guts. The world is just so, so wrong sometimes.

'That's great, Toby.' How can I say this so he will think I mean it but also that it's no big deal to me and then shut up and go away and never say another word about it in my presence?

'They reckon it could be on-going.'

In your dreams, Toby, in your dreams. And here it comes. Here it comes. 'They're bringing me back, actually.'

Toby stops dead in his tracks. 'They're bringing you back?'

Of course I knew I was making a mistake. As soon as I opened my mouth I knew it was the dumbest thing to say. But sometimes short-term victory outweighs long-term defeat. Anyway I'd said it.

'Yeah, well, I haven't finally decided but . . .' I narrowed my eyes and did the dimples.

Toby started going bananas. 'They're bringing you back? The King? The King is coming back?' He stopped boxing and grabbed me by the arms. 'All right! My man!' He was trying to dance me around the optometrist's. I had to get out of there. I called the sales guy.

'I'll take the Vuarnets.'

One thing I am religious about is physical exercise. Okay, say what you like but you just better hope you look like me when you're thirty-eight. People say I'm frivolous. But I'm not. I just work very hard in unorthodox areas. I go to the gym, I eat the right food. I run. Maybe you think you can start at the gym and get to where I am any time you like. Wrong. There are two kinds of people who go to the gym. The people who are striving to perfect the body, and the people who are striving to maintain the body. It is a line which is only crossed in one direction, and once you have crossed this line, you will never ever cross back again. I am thirty-eight and you know what side I'm on? Think about it.

In the gym I was thinking about things. Why not? Why shouldn't I go back? Things were happening. This was the time. The time was ripe. I could hear myself in one of those documentaries in thirty years time (don't ask me why but in the documentary I have a German accent): 'Und zen it vas zat I realised zat I *should*, I *must* go beck to *Paradise Cove*. Zo at ze time it vas merely a choke!' (laughs, and dissolves into fit of coughing). There is after all that strange delicate interplay between what you think is happening and what is happening. I do not, repeat do not, believe in the power of positive thought. But interplay—maybe.

Jamie was waiting when I picked him up. I always make a point of going right into the classroom and saying hi to the teacher. If you can foster some sort of relationship with the people who are dealing with your kid all day, so much the better. Mrs Trevalyan was okay. I think she liked Jamie. She never actually said as much, but reading between the lines, I think she did.

'I'm going to be away for the weekend. Dad's got a job.' We were in the car.

'What job will you do?'

'I'm going to be in an advertisement on TV.'

'Can I watch TV when we get home?'

'After you've done your homework.' We have exactly the same conversation every afternoon. One day, he's sure, he will get to watch TV before he does his homework.

'But you might be in the ad on TV and I might miss it.'

'Don't pick your nose, Jamie.'

'Are you ever going to be in *Paradise Cove* again, Dad?'

'Maybe.'

'Mrs Trevalyan says *Paradise Cove* is rubbish and we shouldn't watch it.'

'Don't pick your nose, Jamie.'

'You pick your nose.'

'I do not.'

'Yes you do.'

'I don't.'

'You do.' The worst thing about children is they're always right.

'Only when I forget. And anyway that's no reason for you to do it.'

'Will you bring me a present?'

'Yes, but only a small one.'

'Why?'

'Because two days isn't very long.'

'How long is two days?'

'It's . . . two days.' He was still looking out the window. 'What are you looking at?'

'Cars.'

'Jamie, don't pick your nose.'

'I forgot.'

When I got home, the tickets were waiting on the kitchen table, still in their courier bag. I realised it was really happening. Tomorrow I would fly to the other end of the country. Someone else would pick Jamie up from school. This was practically the first time in two years it wouldn't be me. Except for the Day of the Parcel.

I had to go back to the hospital that night, so I said goodbye to the kids before I went. I'd be up before them in the morning.

'Lizzie, Daddy's going away for the weekend.'

'Oh . . . why?'

'Daddy has to work.'

'Play ring-a-ring-a-rosy.'

'Daddy doesn't want to play ring-a-ring-a-rosy.'

'Why?'

'Ah . . .'

'Come on, it will be fun.'

I played ring-a-ring-a-rosy.

'. . . all jump up with a one two three!'

I picked her up. 'It's all right, Lizzie,' I said. 'Everything's going to be all right.' She looked at me like I'd just said, 'the sky is blue' or 'rain falls down'.

'Again, Daddy, again.'

Kids.

When I got to the hospital, my sister was by the bed. She looked up and smiled, and I sat down. I looked at the old man. He looked at me. He levered himself up on his pillow and we helped him to sit up. He was looking at me with this intense far-away expression. He wanted to say something to me. He beckoned to me, his dry lips struggling. I leaned forward, straining to hear. It was just exactly like one of those scenes where the dying father whispers his final words into the ear of his son before falling back, dead, on the pillow. I leaned closer.

'Fish tubes.' He said it very slowly and distinctly. He lay back on the pillows looking very pleased with himself. Not at all dead.

'Hi, Dad,' I said. He raised his eyebrows, brought up his hand and stared at his thumb, like he was reading it. I looked at my sister.

'He's been talking about them a lot. Apparently they don't cross the pond properly and he's worried there won't be enough food for the expedition.'

'The expedition?'

'We're climbing Mount Cook, I think. I think we're on the Hochstetter Ice Fall and there's some heavy weather coming in. But we're going for the summit.'

'We?'

'You, me, Jason. We're all there.'

I leant down again. 'Dad,' I said, 'I'm going away for a couple of days. I have a job. In Queenstown. Remember Queenstown, Dad? Remember when you took us down there? Remember that storm? In the mountains? Queenstown. I'm going down there. To work. I have work. I have a job.'

He looked at me. 'Gubble,' he said. I got up to go and I kissed him on the forehead. He was hot and dry. 'Goodbye,' he said.

'I'll be back soon, I'll see you when I get back, I'll see you on Monday.'

'Goodbye,' he said. 'Goodbye.'

'I'll see you on Monday.'

'Where's the primus?'

I should have walked out then and there, but I didn't. I leaned down again. 'Dad,' I said. 'Don't worry, Dad. Everything's all right. Everything's going to be all right.' I took a breath. 'I'm going to make lots of money. I'm going back on *Paradise Cove*.'

'Gubble,' he said.

My sister smiled. 'Dalton,' she said, 'that's wonderful.' She looked relieved, and proud of me, and something else—almost scared. Like maybe I was going to walk out the door and not come back, or not even that, like I wasn't the same. Like . . . I don't know what. I realised she was looking at me the way she used to look at me, before, when I was Dalton Frame. The way a lot of people used to look at me. I mean, people used to look at me. Look at me, hell, they used to watch me.

Sam was in bed when I got home. I climbed in beside her and listened to her breathing. It was awake breathing.

'Jamie says you're going back on *Paradise Cove*.' She said it kind of jokingly, the way you do when you're testing something out because you really want it but maybe you won't get it. This is the part where I really start to sweat it. I mean it started out of this crazy moment and it was taking over my life, but the sweat was, I liked it. The short term was taking over.

'Yeah, it's possible.' It was possible. That's what I was thinking, and it was. It was possible. Make it happen and your lie will never be. It will never even have been a lie, it will melt away, you will reach back in time and erase it. Yes, you will be in *Paradise Cove* again. Your sister will fear you again.

'I'm pregnant.'

I was surprised. I was very, very surprised.

'Dalton?'

Oooh.

'Sweetheart?'

We could not afford this pregnancy.

'Are you okay?'

'That's wonderful, sweetheart,' I said. 'That's so wonderful.' And it was, by God, it was.

'I was thinking,' she said, 'maybe I could stop work.'

'Sure,' I said. 'Sure you could.'

The way the silence settled, I knew that wasn't all.

'What?'

No return.

'What?' Second service.

'It's nothing.'

'I'll be the judge of that.'

'I didn't want to say, with your dad and everything.'

'Say.'

'I didn't want to add to your worries.'

'Add.'

She sighed a long cold sigh. 'Lisa and Barry have split up.'

'Jesus, what is it with these people? All our friends are divorcing.'

'I didn't want to tell you.'

And then she starts crying again.

'Sweetheart?'

There was something else. I knew it. I just knew it.

Sam called me a taxi while I shoved some socks into a bag. We said goodbye on the front step. The children were still asleep but I'd kissed them. Kids are like toast.

'Take care.'

We kissed.

'Take care.'

The taxi took off and I still had it, this feeling.

When I found 12B, I discovered I was seated between two beautiful girls. One was blonde and blue-eyed with a small nose. The other had milk chocolate skin and high cheekbones. This was not a coincidence. Not long after I sat down, one of them leaned across me to the other one and said, 'Where's number three?' And she answered, 'I don't know her, but we're picking her up on the way down.' 'Is she ex-Wellington?' asked the first girl. 'Yah,' said the second. She had this slightly strange way of talking.

'Excuse me . . .' They both turned in to look at me. I couldn't decide which one to look at so I talked to the seat back in front of me. 'You wouldn't be Funky Girls One and Two, would you?' For a moment they were flummoxed but then the one on my left, in the window seat, (milk chocolate) smiled. 'Unhip Street Guy. Right?'

I smiled. 'Dalton. Dalton Frame.' Since it was she who had answered, I looked at her. I found myself blushing. Great beauty of a particular kind has this effect on me. The particular beauty in question is the ephemeral beauty of youth. It's not sexy. No, really. It can't be because it doesn't even know it's there, and by the time it does, it's gone. It's a spiritual thing.

'I'm Marsha, and this is Joanna.'

'Hi,' said Joanna. 'Actually I'm Funky Girl Three. We're picking Two up in Wellington.' We shook hands. I was wishing they'd recognise me because that way at least I would be somebody other than Unhip Street Guy. I mean I know it's acting and all that but who wants to be Unhip Street Guy when you're talking to Funky Girls One and Three? Where is a stewardess when you need her? They were really nice girls and I relaxed, immediately after take off. The only thing I hate more than taking off is landing. Marsha was doing graphic design and modelling part time. Joanna modelled too, but she really wanted to be an actress. They were so nice, I didn't even mind that. Yes, Joanna, I thought to myself. And you might even be an actress one day, who knows?

Wellington airport—I don't know, I just don't understand how it is that they do it time after time and no one gets killed. Marsha noticed my knuckles and was very kind to me. She was a very kind young woman. Very kind and very beautiful. We had about half an hour in Wellington so we went to the bar. I was sweating it. I really didn't want to get back on that plane. I had a beer, Joanna had a mineral water and Marsha had orange juice. We played a game: Spot the Funky Girl. I won, it was child's play. She was over by the magazine shop; tall, flaming red hair. Just as beautiful as the other two. Her name was Diane and she was a dancer. We all got on as if we'd known one another all our lives. That's how it goes, you know you're going to be working together, so for as long as it lasts, you're family. Diane had a low calorie ginger beer, and I had another Beck's. This was a mistake because it got bumpy coming into Queenstown. I might as well come straight out and admit we're talking sick bags here. Marsha was very nice to me. She was getting to be my favourite because she was less daunting than the other two. I felt I could tell Marsha things. Her lower lip was very reassuring.

We landed okay, although Queenstown is another approach I do not recommend. I got off the plane and I was feeling as sick as a dog. Susan met us at the terminal—she'd flown down the day before. The girls went off to look for their bags but Susan beckoned to me to wait behind. There was a guy standing a little way off behind Susan. He looked about twelve. He was this pale hairless little guy, about four foot three (yes I'm exaggerating), with these bandy little legs and pale, pale blue eyes and a tiny little nose with nostrils you could see into, like Nosferatu, and a baseball cap. It was the baseball cap that gave him away. It was the director.

I had, technically, met Bud the director before, at the audition. But he was an American director which means all you saw of him was a bunch of equipment—monitors and tape decks and stuff—and way up the back behind it all a baseball cap sticking up from behind a monitor. Under the baseball cap, you knew, there was a director. Sometimes you heard phrases or comments floating out from under the baseball cap, like 'get him to move to the right two inches' and then the assistant director would ask you to move to the right two inches only you already had because you overheard the baseball cap, so when the assistant moved you another two inches that made four and you had to move back two again.

So this was the first time I had actually laid eyes on the director. I didn't know whether to pick him up in my arms and feed him chicken soup or drive a stake through his heart.

'Dalton, this is Bud. Bud, this is Dalton.'

'Hey, Dalton.'

'Hey, Bud.'

Bud looked at the floor, the tarmac, Susan, the ceiling, Susan, the walls, Susan and back to the floor again. Anything but me. Have you noticed how if anyone ever tells you someone is going to love you they always hate you?

*

The hotel was pretty good. We were right by the lake, close to the restaurants and the outdoor equipment shops. Oh God those outdoor equipment shops. Streets of them. Driving past in the minivan, I got goose flesh. It was heaven—food outlets, liquor shops and outdoor equipment emporiums.

There was a wind on the lake whipping the waves up. The mountains were behind the lake. It was late spring and there was snow on the tops.

In the lobby there was a guy at the check-in. He was checking in. He turned around.

'Toby.'

'Dalton, you old bastard. You aren't on this job too? Jesus I quit, I resign.' He turned to the girls with an arm around me. 'See this guy? Hell to work with.' The girls smiled. The longer I stood with this guy's arm around my shoulders the more of what little mana I had was seeping into the carpet. 'You know who this guy is?' said Toby. They looked puzzled. 'This guy,' said Toby, 'is Dalton Frame. *The* Dalton Frame. The Dalt Man. You know, off *Paradise Cove*.' The girls looked closer. Seconds passed. I wanted to die. Slowly, understanding dawned on the face of Diane, who must have been a microsecond older than the other two. Twice their age, in other words.

'Oh yeah, you played that smooth dick head. What was his name?'

'He's coming back,' said Toby. 'Dalton and me both. We're going to be in Paradise together.'

It was all too tragic for words. I had to change the subject fast. I tore myself out of his grip.

'What are you doing on this job, Toby?'

'Unhip Street Guy Two.'

'There's an Unhip Street Guy Two?' This was news to me.

'You're Unhip Street Guy One?'

'Well, yeah.'

'Hey, my man!' Toby decided to be my body guard. He stood behind me while I checked in. He tried to carry my bag but I wouldn't let him. I headed for my room and he followed. I looked back as I left the lobby and I could see Marsha chatting with Susan and the other girls. I wished there was some way I could talk to Marsha alone. Toby was still being my body guard, saying things like 'you want that I should get you a goil?' and pretending to head butt invisible people. There was a maid coming down the corridor and she looked at us like we were nuts. Toby loved it. When we got to my room he followed me in. He flung himself on the bed, grabbed the remote and turned on the TV. 'Hey watch this, they've got four porn channels. I tell you this is a sweet little number, this job.'

Susan knocked on the door. 'Call sheets for tomorrow. What are you doing tonight?' I looked at Toby, sprawled on my bed. I looked back at Susan. 'Nothing.'

'Come to dinner. Bud's having a few people up to the chalet.'

The chalet was very impressive. It was very big. (I think it was owned by a magnate. A magnate of what, I never discovered. Probably a money-magnate.) The ground floor was a huge studio space, and above it was a mezzanine level with no railing. No railing at all. A staircase that wound up to it from the ground floor had no railing. A kind of window looking down from the bedroom into the central well of the studio also had no railing, no glass, nothing. It all looked very clean and uncluttered but it scared the hell out of me. Releasing a child in it would have been tantamount to attempted murder. The floor was parquet, which I personally detest but, what can you say, it costs a fortune. The furniture, the fittings, the bits and pieces, the lavatory brush, were all Alessi. Alessi I like. There were some blue stained-glass windows way up high, and below them at the studio level plate glass looking out over the lake and across to the mountains. The mountains looked right back.

'Nice view.' Susan was standing behind me. I was looking at the mountains.

'I've been up there.'

'You?' she started that laughing business again.

'Yeah. Why not?'

'You just seem like such a lounge lizard.'

'There's a whole side to me you've never seen.'

She just smiled.

We were drinking Grolsch. It's a good beer. We were sitting on leather couches. I kept slipping off towards the parquet. There were about ten people there, but at one point, Bud and I, uncomfortably, found ourselves alone. Bud finally gave in and talked to me. He leaned forward. He zeroed in on me with his pale blue eyes. 'Your role is absolutely essential to the impact of this commercial.'

I broke into a light sweat. 'Uh-huh.' I nodded earnestly and tried to look very, very serious. Fortunately, very, very serious is a look I do pretty well.

Now then. If you're an actor or you ever want to be one, learn this rule. Learn it from me now. Never, ever, ever, talk to the director. Never. Fake a blackout or an epileptic fit, whatever it takes. But if you aren't a good enough actor for that, or it's against your religion or whatever, then just follow this simple rule. Look the director in the eye. Nod. Look very, very serious. You cannot look too serious. But this is the vital thing: *Do not listen to one single word he or she is saying.* Because anything he or she says to you, will come back and haunt you and fuck you up forever, for the rest of your life. And the rest of your life is a long, long time. Believe me, I know what I'm saying.

'The fact that you have only four seconds of screen time to achieve that impact makes it all the more important that every second counts.'

'Right.' Four seconds?

'What we've got, we've got the girls, right? Clowning around, doing their thing. Having fun. And you are the catalysing event.'

'The catalysing event.'

'You are the male gaze.'

'The male gaze.'

'That's right, the male gaze. You have this perfect gaze, perfect for that. That's why you were cast.'

'That's why I was cast.' (I'm employing an additional technique here which I'll explain later.)

'What I mean to say is, you're ambiguous. You're sexy but unwholesome.'

'Unwholesome.'

'What we see here is a sexy but unwholesome presence. The sexiness of the presence empowers the girls, it bestows sexual attractiveness and power on them.'

'Sexual attractiveness and power.'

'Right. They are attractive, because they attract. But the unwholesomeness, this is the key. The unwholesomeness unites them against the male gaze. It unifies them, it gives them tribehood.'

'Tribehood.'

'Tribehood.'

'Tribehood.'

What I'm doing is this: I'm repeating what he says. But—and here is the skill of it—I am still *not listening to a single word he says*. That takes practice, but it can be done.

'Yes. Tribehood. It creates out of these three girls the Girl Tribe. And so the quality of sexual empowerment is coupled with a sense of belonging, and these are the qualities we wish to associate with the product. That's the essence.'

'The essence.'

Commercial directors don't seem to understand that they're making crap and they're doing it for the money. It's funny, they just don't seem to have noticed that everybody hates commercials and they're crap. Of course you might say, hey what about the commercial directors who have gone on to make fine movies? Ridley Scott, I believe, is one such director. However, a more pertinent question would surely be: how many feature film directors have gone on to make fine commercials? Anyway.

'Does that make sense to you?' Bud is already leaning forward, but he leans forward a little more.

'That makes sense to me.'

'We've got a really exciting commercial here. We're all very excited.'

'Very excited.'

'Great. I'm glad you feel that way.'

'You're glad I feel that way.'

The bathroom was my absolute favourite bathroom. White tiles on the walls and ceiling, and black and white tiled floor. It's the perfect bathroom—no matter what happens it'll be easy to clean up, and if you're in there for a long time you can always play chess. There was also a floor-to-ceiling mirror. I eyeballed myself. I really eyeballed myself, and I didn't flinch once. The Grolsch certainly helped. Looking closer, however, I discerned a certain bitterness towards myself which I hadn't expected to see. This was not an appealing sight. I wiggled my eyebrows at myself to try to snap myself out of it but it didn't work; I just stared back at myself with a look that said it all: shit was going down. And that's fair enough, it was. On the other hand, there's no need to lose your sense of humour.

Susan and the director were talking when I got back. 'Dalton is writing a screenplay,' said Susan, playfully.

'What sort of screenplay?'

'Science fiction,' I said. 'Kind of social comment.'

'I love science fiction.' Susan was trying to help. I could see that.

'Pitch me,' said the director.

'I don't pitch.'

Susan looked at me with this look, and I thought, Oh Christ she's probably just got back from Sundance. 'If you don't pitch you're not a writer,' she said, and wagged her finger. She was right. I didn't pitch and I wasn't a writer.

'Okay,' I said, 'I'll pitch you. But I don't normally do this. So . . . I warned you.' Bud shifted uneasily. 'Okay . . . there's this guy.'

'Great start.' Susan was being just a little bit too helpful.

'There's this guy, and he works at a sewage pond. A sewage treatment station.'

'What does he do there?'

'He, ah . . . he controls the outward flow of sewage. It's his job to make sure the sewage ponds are always full but never overflowing.'

'Important job.'

'Oh yes. He takes his job very seriously. Anyway, one day his best friend, who also works at the sewage station, is found dead and mangled, floating in one of the ponds.'

'Gross.'

'I should warn you I'm thinking Peter Jackson here.'

'Hasn't he kind of moved on?'

'Maybe. Probably. Anyway, his friend is found floating mangled in the sewage treatment ponds . . . and he's been fucked up the arse. Or so it seems.' Susan's smile wavered, like a candle in a draught. Bud sat up straighter and sucked on his beer. 'So, he's really upset about this.' Bud was listening now. I tried not to look at him. Those blue eyes. 'Very upset. But he's also very suspicious. He suspects an inside job. He knows that his friend went back to the treatment station the night he died—he was getting married the next day and he left his fiancée's engagement ring in his locker at work.'

'Nice touch.'

'It's full of nice touches.'

'And I assume he was going to be the best man?'

'He was.'

'Does he get together with the fiancée?'

'Do you want to tell this?'

'No, no, go on.'

'So anyway the friend—'

'The dead one?'

'The live one, our guy, our man.'

'Sorry.'

'He's really upset, and the police don't have any clues so he starts sniffing around, you know, looking for clues.'

'Like you do.'

'Like you do. And he finds out, quite by chance—like he's sneaking round the station at night, right, looking for clues—and he sees the lights on in the manager's office and he sneaks up to the window and looks in and sees the manager, and as he watches, the manager removes his head, and reveals—'

'Removes whose head?'

'His own, the manager's. The manager removes his own head. And underneath he's just got this vile snake-like, tongue-like organ. He's an alien. Blah blah. Special effects. Peter Jackson.'

'Sounds like *Men in Black*.'

'Only this is really gross. So anyway, he's freaked out, and he goes to the police.'

'A mistake?'

'A mistake.'

At this point Susan got up and went to the fridge. The word 'mistake' was ringing in my ears. Bud sat back. His eyes were getting bluer. I plunged ahead.

'So he goes to the police and tells them the manager is an

alien with a huge tongue-like organ where his head should be, and of course they immediately arrest him and charge him with the murder of his friend. And yes he has been comforting the fiancée, who is told by the police that it was some sort of jealousy thing as the guy and his friend were obviously lovers. Etcetera. So he gets away, and he's on the run.'

'How does he get away?' I wasn't sure if Bud was talking to me or his beer bottle.

'I don't know, he gets away, he strangles a guard.'

'The fiancée should help him.'

'You two have got a real thing about this fiancée.'

'Dimensionalises the characters.'

'These are not dimensional characters.'

'All characters are dimensional.'

'Even in Pepsi ads?' This was possibly the dumbest thing I have ever said in my life. Bud looked at me. His eyes blazed blue, blue, blue. I hurried on. 'Actually, you know, that's not a bad idea. The fiancée strangles the guard. I like it. It is more dimensional. So anyway he's on the run, with the fiancée, and he goes to the manager's place to try to catch him and prove that he's an alien. Cos he figures this is his only chance. So he breaks into the manager's house, but he gets caught. And the manager explains to him that . . .'

'Explanations are boring.'

'Not this one. The manager explains that, in fact, what's going on is this. The human race has been bred, like cattle. We are being farmed for a product we produce in abundance.' I took a swig and smiled. 'Shit.'

Susan was back. Bud smirked. He looked up at her, back at me. 'Shit, as in doo-doos? As in ka-ka?'

'Yup. Excrement. On other planets, human excrement is a hallucinogenic substance of incredible power and value. But it's also a forbidden substance. The aliens who are farming the planet seeded Earth with the first rudimentary organisms, cultivated and subtly guided humans to develop the civilisation we now have, with the biology and the culture we now have, for one reason only: so that we would of our own volition build and maintain sewage systems which collect and concentrate excrement for collection and exploitation by the farmer-aliens. That's what UFOs are up to. They're like the rural milk tanker. And of course it's not accidental that the substance that is making them rich is the substance humans value least of all. Makes us far less likely to ask questions. We never wonder where our sewage really goes. All we care about is that we don't see it again.'

'How does it end?'

'He escapes.'

'Again?'

'Again, with or without the fiancée. He kills the manager, big fight, chase sequence etcetera. And he makes his way to Paris.'

'Paris?'

'Paris. He hides out in the sewers, and by a unique twist of fate becomes the saviour of mankind.'

'How does he manage that?'

'He finds out how to get in touch with the galactic police. Steals a sub-etheric transmitter from the manager's place. He sets up a signal which will notify the galactic police that there is an illegal shit farm operating in the Sol region. If they get this message of course the galactic police will destroy the planet. He uses this threat to force a few concessions out of the aliens: a cure for cancer, an end to world hunger and so on. The Millennium arrives. Heaven on Earth.'

'But wouldn't it be in the aliens' interests to keep us healthy anyway?'

'Look at the conditions they keep pigs in. It's economics. The way things are it costs them nothing at all to run the place. All they have to do is harvest the shit. Oh, but food is important. And guess what food produces the highest quality shit? Fast food of course. Maybe I'll set it twenty years in the future, when everyone eats nothing but McDonald's, drinks nothing but Pepsi.'

'But what sort of a threat is it to the aliens that you'll destroy our own planet?'

'It's a game of chicken. If Earth is destroyed, the aliens lose their investment, whereas world peace and happiness is a little more expensive than the status quo, but a perfectly sustainable dent in the profit margins. So as long as he can convince them he's crazy enough to do it, they'll do business.'

Susan laughed nervously. 'You're a joker, Dalton.'

'I left out the grossest part. You know how his friend was fucked up the arse . . . ?'

Susan laughed again. 'I don't need to hear it.'

Bud interrupted. 'Yeah, what about it?'

'Well, you know how nice it is to drink milk straight from the cow?'

Bud grinned at his beer bottle. He shook his head, slowly. His eyes were dull and distant. Silence settled. Heavily.

Susan broke it. 'Some time though you will have to tell us your idea.'

I just had. She laughed again, uneasily. 'He's such a joker.'

Bud stood up and stretched. 'Explanations are boring.' He wandered off.

Susan watched him go. 'He's such a perfectionist. You know he doesn't really want to make commercials.'

'You're kidding!'

'But he just can't find a good enough script. For ten years now he's been searching for a script good enough to make.'

'He must have started looking before he was potty-trained.'

'He's older than he looks.'

'Maybe he just wouldn't know a good script if it bit him

on the arse.' I was feeling bitter, I admit it. That was a damn good idea for a film I'd just pitched him. A damn good pitch too. Susan looked at me like I'd just expressed a desire to violate the Virgin Mary.

Susan walked me back to the hotel. 'So, how's your father?'

'The end is imminent.'

'Are you sure you feel okay about coming down here?'

'It's not that imminent.'

'It's hard to tell with these things I guess.'

'Pretty hard.'

'It must be hard for you.'

'He's in no pain. That's a good thing.'

'I'm so sorry,' she said.

'Don't worry about it.'

'If there's ever anything I can do . . .'

'Thanks.' Our eyes met and unfortunately the barrier was down. That's all I can say. It just was. Normally with someone like Susan I'd be looking at her from the parapet, from behind the wire. We'd both know it and that's how we'd look. But this time I looked and it just wasn't there. It was like missing the top of the stairs. You step and there's nothing there.

'I was telling Jamie you'd be down here.' When in situations like this, always talk about your children.

'He's a beautiful boy.'

'Yes, he is.'

'Takes after his dad.'

I left that lying. Tactically clumsy. Take it and run with it, or kick it into touch, but don't just leave it lying there.

Susan changed tack. 'I hear you're going back on *Paradise Cove*.'

'Where did you hear that?'

'I have my sources.'

'I'm thinking about it.'

'I've been thinking about you lately, Dalton.' Where was that guide rope? Where was the barrier? 'I've been remembering that time on the beach . . .'

On the beach? What beach? And then I remembered. 'Oh my God . . .' It came to me in a blinding flash of total erotic recall. Susan. Susan . . . that Susan. Seven years ago. The wrap party. The sunrise. The cocaine. The beach. The trees. The blanket. Her hair was completely different. It is utterly incredible what you can forget if you put your mind to it. That Susan, that Susan, *that Susan*. Oh Lord oh Jesus. Mother of God. I was alone on the mountainside, the cold wheeling stars my only witness, face to face with my own sexual Armageddon. She was incredible. Her eyes were full of stars. She moved closer to me. I'm weak. I'm weak.

'Jamie . . .' I croaked.

'Jamie thinks we're going to fall in love.'

'Sam . . .'

But she only moved closer. Her eyes were glistening. 'I'm sorry. I don't want to fuck anything up for you, Dalton, I just can't help it . . . ever since I saw you again . . . I just wish you'd . . .'

So this was how it happened. This was how all those hapless couples split, sundered, divided, divorced.

My cell phone rang. Susan hovered, inches away. I answered.

'H-hello?'

There was a strange snuffling noise at the other end and for one bizarre moment I thought I was being telephoned by a dog.

'Hello?'

'It's me.'

'Sam?'

'Dalton. Your dad. He died.'

It's such a moment, that, in any man's life. I think I could say without fear of exaggeration that it's a defining moment. I remember the scene very clearly. I remember Susan standing in front of me, inches away, her eyes on mine, her face so close it was distorted like a fish-eye lens. I remember the sky behind her. The stars crowding together, jostling for a clear view, so many of them because it was so dark. So many stars.

Susan drew back. 'Are you okay?'

'That was Sam.' I didn't want to tell her. I didn't want her sympathy.

'Is everything okay?'

'Yeah, everything's okay. My dad died.'

I had to get out of this. I wished Sam was there. I began to walk down the hill. Susan followed. 'Oh my God, Dalton, I'm so sorry . . .'

'That's okay. It's good, it's good. He was only suffering. He's happier now.'

'But you're here and they're there . . . and . . .'

Marsha. I had to see Marsha. I began to walk a little faster. Susan had to break into a jog. I've got long legs. We jog-trotted down the main street of Queenstown, past all the outdoor equipment shops with their plate glass windows, past the restaurants, past the little knots of Japanese tourists, past the parties, spilling out of the bars and into the little streets and squares, the party people, the off-season groovers, the snow-boarders and ski guides and helicopter pilots and jet boaters, the mountain bikers and back packers, young people in flared pants and dreadlocks, with their flat stomachs and eyebrow rings, their nose rings and navel rings, their tight pants and loose shirts, their loose pants and tight shirts, their tongue studs and nipple rings, their lip rings, wedding rings and cock rings, rings within rings, circles in squares. Past the lake. The hotel was all lit up like Christmas.

'Which is Marsha's room?' We were in the corridor. Susan was breathing hard. She looked at me like she hated me and walked away without saying a word. I started knocking on doors. I didn't care any more. The first door was a complete stranger. The second door was Joanna. She told me Marsha was in 131, next door, but she was having a shower. I knocked anyway. Joanna closed her door but she was watching through the crack. Marsha opened her door. She was wrapped in a towel.

'Can I come in?'

She blinked. 'I'm having a shower.'

Joanna came back out into the hall. I was starting to sweat. Marsha was looking embarrassed and angry. She went to close the door.

'My father died.'

She stopped. 'What, now?'

'Just now. I just got a call.' I held up my cell phone, to prove it.

Joanna took a step forward. 'Oh dear,' she said.

Susan was coming back again, down the hall. Her cheeks were red. Toby appeared behind her, coming from my room. Fake orgasms and musak drifted faintly out of the open door.

'What's going on?' said Susan.

'His father just died,' said Joanna.

'I know that,' said Susan.

'Hey, where you been?' said Toby. His eyes were as red as Dracula's.

'Please,' I said to Marsha.

Crying is not what everyone thinks. I mean this is coming from a guy who hadn't cried since he was ten. Directors have wept, trying to get me to cry. And yes, I always thought that to cry is unmanly. And yes, I think a man should be manly. If he can. But crying is a blast. Crying is a dream. It's not exactly sexy, but it's a release, it's a gushing, it's a pouring forth. It feels fantastic, it must be the endorphins. And the other thing is, people don't mind it at all. They don't get embarrassed or pissed off. They love it. It makes them feel all tender and public-spirited. Marsha made a decision. She grabbed my arm, pulled me into the room. She pulled back the covers on the bed. 'Get in.' I got in. 'Lie down.' I lay down. 'Stay there.' I curled up and shut my eyes. Boo hoo. Boo hoo. It was warm and dark. Boo hoo. It was all right. Boo. Marsha was there. Hoo. I think I fell asleep.

I could hear people moving about the room. I could hear whispered conversation.

'There's some tea bags here.'

'I'll put the jug on.'

'I think he's asleep.'

I opened my eyes. They were all there. Joanna, Diane and Marsha. Marsha was dressed now.

'He's awake,' said Joanna.

I had no idea how long it had been. They all came to sit on the end of the bed, and looked at me sympathetically. It was like being in *Charlie's Angels*. 'Cup of tea?' said Joanna. There was a knock at the door. Diane went to answer. I heard Susan's voice, then Diane's. Diane came back into the room.

'Susan wants to know what you're going to do.'

'I'm going to have a cup of tea.'

Diane went back to the door. The voices were more agitated this time. She came back.

'Susan says she needs to know what you're doing.'

'Tell her to talk to my agent.'

Diane went back. The jug began to make noises. Marsha got up and poured four cups of tea. I could hear Susan's voice in the corridor: she sounded pretty upset. Marsha called out to Diane, 'Milk and sugar?' and Diane called back, 'Milk, no sugar.' Joanna opened a packet of biscuits. I'm telling you all this because I have complete recall for every tiny thing that happened in that room. Weird. I can play it like a movie any time I like.

Diane came back. 'I really think you need to talk to Susan.'

Susan was standing behind her. I sat up in bed a little. 'Cup of tea?'

'I'm sorry about your dad, Dalton.'

'Thank you.'

'But I need to know if you're working tomorrow.' Susan was looking stressed. She had red spots on her cheekbones and her eyes were a little wild. I took a sip of tea. 'Listen.' She moved closer. 'I'll tell you something I wasn't going to tell you. Bud wasn't sure about you for this part . . .'

'Who's Bud?'

'The director, Dalton. The director. You just had dinner with him.'

'Oh, him.'

'I went out on a limb for you. I talked them into giving you this job. I told them what a great actor you are. I told them with your reputation you'd give the commercial gravitas.'

'Gravitas? I thought it was unwholesomeness.'

'Unwholesomeness?' This was Marsha.

'Yeah, Bud was telling me just this evening, I'm sexy but unwholesome.'

'You're not unwholesome.'

'God bless you.'

'He's not unwholesome is he?' Marsha appealed to the girls.

'No way,' said Joanna.

'He is kind of sexy in a way though,' said Diane, grudgingly. 'I mean for a particular age group.'

'*Excuse me.*' Susan was now looking seriously stressed. She moved between me and the girls. 'This is a conversation between me and Dalton. Would you all mind leaving for a minute?'

'Well excuse *me*,' said Diane, 'but this is Marsha's room

and I don't think you should be hassling a guy whose father died just half an hour ago.'

'I am the producer on this commercial, and I am paying for this hotel room and I'm asking you to give me ten minutes alone with Dalton.'

'Anything you say to me you can say in front of them.'

Susan sighed. She sat on the end of the bed. 'Then at least shut up. Now look, Dalton, if you feel you just can't make it, or if you need to get back home, I understand. I really do. But I need to know now. I need to try to organise someone else by tomorrow morning. My arse is on the line here.'

Toby was standing in the doorway. He'd been listening. 'Hey, I don't want to interrupt or anything but if Dalton can't do it I'm available. To do his line, I mean.'

In your dreams, Toby. 'Of course I'm working.'

Susan looked at me. 'Are you sure?'

'The show must go on.' With the girls about me, a cup of tea in my hand, the way was clear. The show did have to go on. I was going to do this job, and do it brilliantly. I would do it for Dad. I got up. 'Now if you'll excuse me,' I said, 'I have to go and work on my lines.' Before I left the room I stopped to shake Marsha by the hand. 'Thank you,' I said. 'You might just have saved my life.'

I rang Sam when I got back to my room. She said everyone was coping fine and the funeral was on Monday. The kids were still up, and very excited. She put Jamie on. He wanted to know if Grandad would be at the funeral. I said he would be, but Jamie wouldn't see him because he would be in a box. Jamie wanted to be in the box too. I said the box was just for Grandad. He wanted his own box. I said he'd have to wait.

'Till Christmas?'

'A little longer than that.'

'Ohh . . .'

Then Sam put Lizzie on. Lizzie breathed down the line. I sang her a little song.

'Ring-a-ring-a-rosy, a pocket full of posies . . .'

Lizzie breathed.

'Lizzie?'

(Breathing.)

'Is that you darling?'

(Heavy breathing.)

'Take good care of Mummy.'

Lizzie had the most beautiful breath in the world. I was going to do that part. I was going to do it for my children's breath, and the breath of their children, and the breath of my children's children's children, and for all the breath my dad had ever breathed and would never breathe. By now I was feeling fantastic. I was on a high. Grief is the most closely guarded secret of them all. We, the grievers, don't want you to know. We can't tell you because we don't understand ourselves. And anyway, everyone gets a turn. I was on a high, but I was suffering. I was in torment, I was a Greek tragedy. I was catharsis. It was all the endorphins. I had a shower. Toby knocked on the door.

'Hey, boss, thought you might like this.' He flashed a joint at me, sauntered through, flopped onto my bed and put the porn channel on again. We smoked the joint while he told me a long story about some job he almost got and he could probably sue them if he wanted. Appropriately enough, the porn movie was called *The Audition*.

'Sue them,' I said. 'Sue the bastards.'

I wondered if Dad made it up the icefall. There was another knock at the door. I turned off the TV.

'Hey!' said Toby. 'I was watching that.'

I crossed the room, which seemed to take a long time. I opened the door just a little bit. It was Susan.

'Hi.' She had an apologetic look.

One thing producers do not understand is actors smoking dope. It's fine for them but not for actors. It's kind of like that no-sex-the-night-before-the-game thing for rugby players. Anyway, I didn't want her to see into the room, especially as Toby had turned the TV back on.

'I wanted to say sorry if I came down a bit hard on you.'

'Oh that's fine. No problem.' I was the hero now, the man of the hour. She was trying to see past me into the room, but I kept myself square in the doorway. She was dying to see if it was Marsha. I let her suffer. She shrugged and said she'd see me tomorrow.

'Sure,' I said. She patted me on the cheek and smiled.

'No more wacky-baccy. Your eyes look like a lava flow.'

I finally got rid of Toby about midnight. We'd ordered room service and Toby had told me all about how when your dad dies you shouldn't worry about it because everyone's dad dies. That was a real help.

When he was gone I went to the bathroom and looked in the mirror. Susan was right about the eyes. I practised my lines for tomorrow. 'Hey, hey, hey. Hey, *hey*, hey. *Hey*, hey, hey. Hey, hey, *hey*. Heyheyhey.' One of those. I could decide on the day. I tried to think unwholesome but sexy. The unwholesome was easy. Sexy . . . I thought about Susan, but when all is said and done I have trouble with authority figures. I thought about Marsha but there was just too much unwholesome in it to let the sexy come through. Jesus, I thought, I must be getting old. I went to bed.

As I lay on my back waiting to fall asleep I remembered that Dylan Thomas poem. You know, do not go gently into that good night, something like that. Rage, rage against the dying of the light. That was it, that one. Rage. Rage on, Dad. I thought about Sam. I thought, Godammit, I'll ring her. I whipped out the trusty cell phone. It was a long time ringing. The voice that answered was not Sam's. Nor, indeed, was it

Lizzie's or Jamie's. It was a voice I knew.

'Hello?' said the voice, sounding a little tentative.

I hung up. Stupid thing to do. Totally unnecessary.

I got a wake-up call at five forty-five. It was Susan.

'But I didn't ask for a wake-up call.'

'Today, Dalton, I ride you like a horse.'

At breakfast there were two tables. The girls were at one, Toby was at the other. All by himself. I went over to Toby's table.

'Gidday, boss.'

'Morning, Toby.'

Toby grinned around a mouthful of bacon and eggs. I took a chair from Toby's table and went to join the girls. There wasn't really room but I didn't care. Marsha shoved over. The girls all looked at me.

'How did you sleep?' asked Marsha.

'I slept well, thank you.' They all looked at me like I was a hero. What a brave answer.

After breakfast we had a couple of hours on wardrobe calls with Bud, then we were going out to shoot. The girls went down first, Toby and I were up next. This meant Toby and I had forty minutes or more hanging out together. We weren't to leave our rooms; they wanted us by the phone. Toby said to look for him in my room. He lay on my bed and turned on the porn channel.

'Wanna doobie?'

'No, Toby.' I do have standards. 'And are you planning to *pay* for all these?'

The wardrobe department was set up in another room in the hotel. The girls were still there when we arrived. They were all standing round in hiking boots and hot pants, looking bored. They were utterly sensational. Bud was standing by the window, staring out at the lake and scratching his head under his baseball cap. The wardrobe mistress was carefully examining her nail polish. The atmosphere was tense. The girls all said hi and smiled and filed out past Toby and me. Just as they got to the door, Bud called them back.

'Lemme see the miniskirts again.' The wardrobe mistress sighed. Toby and I sat against the wall and watched as the girls went away and came back, one by one, in miniskirts; a red one, a green one and a gold one. Toby had fallen uncharacteristically silent. Bud's finger stabbed the air. 'Keep *her* in the mini, put *her* and *her* in the hot pants. And change *that* T-shirt for the halter top.' Away they went and back they came. Next it was someone else in the mini, and the other two in hot pants, then one lot of hot pants and two minis. God knows what they'd been doing before we came down. The halter top worked its way round the trio, followed by a lamé boob-tube. Finally they were back in the hot pants again, all three of them. 'All right,' said Bud, 'that's it. That's what I want.' The wardrobe mistress bit her lip. I think she drew blood. Bud finally turned to me. He hadn't even looked at me, let alone said good morning yet.

'Good morning,' I said.

Bud looked at my forehead, then my chest. 'Sorry about your dad.'

'These things happen.'

He nodded. He looked at Toby. 'Get them to swap their T-shirts.' He was talking to the wardrobe mistress but he obviously meant us.

'But these are *our* clothes.' I was wearing what I always wear. Jeans and T-shirt. Same with Toby. The wardrobe mistress looked at me with a pleading expression. I thought what the hell. We swapped T-shirts. Toby's was too small for me and mine was too big for Toby. We looked like total dicks.

'Perfect.' said Bud. He strode out of the room.

*

We were all pretty quiet in the minibus. Susan was driving, the girls were in a row right across the back. Toby was by himself in the middle, I was up front next to Susan. I get car sick. I had wanted to sit next to Marsha but now they were in costume the girls were kind of sticking together. They were talking and walking differently, too. Laughing louder, going around together, striding like they were on a cat walk, and standing with their hips stuck out. That tribehood thing must have been starting to happen. I was thinking about my dad. Looking out the window at all those mountains. Wondering if he made it.

There were a few clouds gathering up behind the mountains on the other side of the lake. We slowly wound higher and higher up a ski access road. The lake opened out below us, and the mountains spread from one horizon to the other. I felt like I was getting closer to him.

Finally we got to where we were going. This was summer, but there was snow around, old snow, last year's snow, lying packed down hard in the dips and gullies. We were way above the bush line and it was mainly rock and dirt, with a scattering of alpine tussock, vegetable sheep and suchlike. The crew was all set up already. The scene was like this. The girls would be on the summit of the mountain, and Toby and I would be struggling up behind them, totally knackered. Just as we got up to them, they'd finish the last of their Pepsi cans, and chuck the cans away. Toby and me would groan and moan and collapse in despair, and then the girls would stride purposefully back down, past our collapsed forms. There were plenty of shots and already time was passing. The first assistant was a guy called Chuck. He had tattoos on his forearms and a heavy metal T-shirt. He sat me and Toby down by the refreshments table and took the girls over for the first shot.

The main thing about filming, any sort of filming, is it is

the most slow-moving activity in the world. The trained professional knows how to deal with the situation. Don't get excited. Stay near the food. Hang out with either the wardrobe person or the makeup person but not the extras. I sat on a fold-out chair and looked across at the mountains. It was clear blue sky where we were but the clouds were still gathering across the lake. They were looking darker. I had my cell phone in my pocket. I kept thinking I should call.

The girls were standing on an outcrop of rock which was supposed to look like the top of the mountain. They were grouped with Joanna at the highest point and the other two sort of aspiring up to her. They looked great. There was a crane and a dolly and tracks and all sorts of shit. They were dollying in and craning up at the same time to get that top-of-the-mountain swoop feeling. Lots of leg too. They'd take the dolly right back along the tracks, and the girls would walk the last few steps, Joanna in the lead, and then the girls would turn and look back down the valley and the dolly would track in, and in, and the crane would sweep up to the sky as the girls held up a can of Pepsi and grinned. Over and over, they did this. Over, and over. The sun was getting high, and hot. They kept coming in with sunscreen for Joanna's nose. The shot was mainly Joanna, and it was a pretty vital shot, and they just kept doing it over and over.

Joanna was amazing, like steel. She never missed a beat, she'd just swing around, look back at the lake, and smile this great smile, and swig that can. Perfect every time. Never missed a mark, never stumbled, a perfect smile every time. It's hard to do, that. Real hard. People don't realise. If you watched without knowing, you'd think nobody was doing anything at all, and whatever they did seem to be doing would look easy as pie. But it's not. There's a million little things to remember; start here and finish here, and do it in this many seconds. Get the Pepsi can to here, just as your feet arrive there. And angle the can so the camera can see the logo. Oh, and remember to SMILE. And look like you're not doing anything at all. I guess it is easy if you can do it, but if you can't do it you just can't. Dancers are usually good at it. It's more like dancing if you ask me. Joanna was great. And only nineteen. So I was watching Joanna do her stuff, and I thought, *I can't do this*.

By the time they'd got that shot, it was getting well on. They did a quick repo for the next shot. They were going to do one more shot then break for lunch about one. Chuck came over. 'You're in, guys.' Chuck looked like he should have been a Vietnam vet, only he was too young. Maybe he was an ex-marine, or a convict. I don't know. He was a good first, because you did exactly what he told you to do very quickly. Toby and I got into position. We were down the hill from the girls—or at least where the girls had been. We had to look up and imagine we were struggling up the hill to get to them. Bud came over to explain.

'Okay, guys. You've been climbing this mountain to get to these girls. They've blasted up this mountain like they're mountain goats. You're footsore, you're weary, you're sweating, you're exhausted. You look up and you see the girls. Then they chuck the can of Pepsi over the crevasse. You look at the girls. You look at the crevasse. You look back at the girls. You charge over to the crevasse. Just like you did in the audition. Okay?'

Chuck launched into action. 'Okay, let's go for a rehearsal. Rehearsing. And . . . action!'

It was that mountain. It was that sky. I don't know what it was. Yes I do. It was the cell phone in my pocket. I was thinking, Why don't you ring? Why don't you give Sam a ring, and just say, really casual, oh, was that John who answered the phone last night? Yeah, I got cut off. Bloody satellite. All perfectly, perfectly, perfectly. What was worst of all was I wasn't doing it, I wasn't ringing her. And who was that? Was that her or me?

A suspicious mind has a guilty conscience. Surprisingly viable, Dalton. What the hell did that mean?

Do you ever think about how small we are? It's impossible to get a handle on, that, unless you happen to be on a mountain. We are just so fucking small. They'd put a guy on top of the rock to pretend to be the girls. He was tiny. He was holding up a can of Pepsi and waving it round. Me and Toby had to look at it and then watch as he chucked it away. The guy waved the can. I could hear Toby sniffling behind me. I watched the guy wave the can. The guy was getting smaller. We were all getting smaller. The sky was getting bigger. Then even the mountain was getting smaller. The sky was opening out. That cell phone was in my pocket. The guy chucked the can. Toby ran past me.

'Cut.' Chuck came over. 'Dalton?'

'Yes, Chuck?'

'You run for the can too, Dalton.'

'Oh yeah, right. Sorry, Chuck. Run for the can.'

'When he throws it, you run for it. Okay, Dalton?'

'Okay, Chuck, when he chucks the can, I run for it. Chuck.'

They set up for another rehearsal. Chuck bent down and had a little chat with Bud, who was hiding behind the monitor.

I ran for it. This time, I ran. It felt good. I'm a good runner. Always kept in shape. The guy chucked the can and I ran. I ran and ran. I ran past the can. I ran past Toby. I saw a surprised look on his face. I ran higher. There was a shout. I think it was Chuck. I didn't turn around. I kept running. I ran straight at the slope. It was like the mountain was rolling back under my feet. I was under the sky and the world was turning. The tiny world. I didn't look back. The cell phone was banging against my thigh.

It took me a little while before I realised where I was running—I was heading for high ground. I was going to keep running until there was nowhere to run but down. All I had to do was just follow the ridge line. There was a rocky bit at one point, and I had to do some scrambling, but not much.

I didn't stop once. I didn't look back. I think I heard some other shouts but they were well behind. I was following the ridge line. The false summit rolled slowly away from me. There's always a false summit, and then another, and then another, and each time you think, This is it at last, but it never is, until finally you stop thinking about ever getting there—and that's just when you do.

I was going hard and at some point it began to hurt. I didn't care. I liked it. The more it hurt the harder I ran. My legs turned to custard but I didn't care about that either.

I knew I was getting close when the air stream hit me from behind. You go up and up and the air is still but at some point you come out of the shelter of the other peaks around you and you've got this steady stream of cold air right between the shoulder blades. I was wearing a down jacket they'd lent me to rehearse in so it didn't feel too bad. The sound was awesome. The teeth of the wind tearing at the rocks. Sometimes it would change direction, come round and biff you on the side of the head.

Just running.

It was when I'd been running for about an hour and a half probably. I was high, the wind was on me. The pain was very strong. I thought, *I'm going to have to stop*. And there he was. He ran with me. I tell you he was there. I don't know what that means but it was true. I don't mean I felt like he was. I mean he *was*. I'm telling you. He ran with me until the pain passed and I could carry on. He ran me over the last false summit and round a big boulder, and there was the top in front of me.

I'd been running a couple of hours. It wasn't a real peak or anything, but I'd followed the spur all the way to where it joined the main ridge line, and it was a high point along the ridge, so the view was fantastic. I could see right over into the next valley, and I could see mountains after mountains after mountains on the other side, rucked up like a huge blanket. There was a little cairn to mark the summit. I added a rock.

I looked back the way I had come. I couldn't see any sign of the crew or the vehicles but there was a line of pursuers strung out behind me. They looked tiny. There were about five or so in all. Across the lake the clouds were boiling, piling up on top of one another. And they were coming this way, fast. They were rain clouds, snow clouds if the temperature kept dropping. The wind was a steady jet stream howling across my ears. My nose stung. The followers had hardly moved. I couldn't tell who they were but then I noticed a bright yellow parka way out in front, way ahead of the others. Whoever it was would be with me long before the main party arrived. I had a wild hope it would be Sam.

A storm in the mountains is like nothing else. They used to think the thunder was giants chucking boulders around—well that's what it sounds like, the whole mountain shakes. My dad and my brother and me were snowed in that time in the mountains. We huddled in that tiny tent while the whole mountain shook. All that night and all the next day and the next night. I've never felt so small. I thought then, and I'd never really thought it before, we could all die out here.

The clouds across the lake were heading this way, fast. It was a race between them and the yellow parka. I sat down to wait.

His Father's Shoes

I spent all last winter I was walking around in a pair of those you know those kung fu shoes just made of flimsy cloth and all falling apart with a big hole in the toe and my feet would get soaked in all the puddles and all cold and wet. I really needed a good pair of shoes. A good pair of leather shoes. Waterproof shoes, comfortable, hard wearing, that I can walk long distances in. That will protect my feet from the road, from sharp objects, from mud and cold.

And my father had this pair of old boat shoes. He didn't wear them on the boat any more, just for gardening. He's got a new pair for the boat. But these are just his old knock-about gardening shoes. He never gardens. They just sit around in the wash-house under the sink.

But they were just what I needed. Exactly what I needed. They fit me, they were well made and comfortable and waterproof. So I made an approach to him at one time, if he would like to give me those shoes. I explained to him that I do a lot of walking and I needed some good leather shoes on my feet. I asked him politely and reasonably. I just quietly asked, or rather if you like I suggested, if I could possibly have or he might like to make a gift to me of those old gardening shoes down in the wash-house.

And his answer was no. Which was typical for him. And so I asked him, quite politely and reasonably, for his reason for refusing, and he said that they had sentimental value. His exact words were: 'I'd rather not, they have a certain sentimental value, you see.'

Sentimental value.

I decided to pursue this whole question of sentiment, of feeling, of emotional attachment, because I felt that I had a lot to say to him about this subject. There was a lot that I wanted to say to him. And what I wanted to suggest to him here was that there might be, perhaps, a greater sentimental value to him in the act of giving his son something he needs, in giving him a pair of shoes, than in denying that son a pair of shoes just for the sake of having this old pair of worn-out boat shoes sitting around under the house.

But I did also want to make it clear to him that I wasn't angry or upset, that I was just picking up, pursuing this theme in the spirit of a spirited or you might even say a high-spirited or almost humorous although at the same time not entirely frivolous debate, but not at all acrimonious, just to say, just to point it out to him, so first of all to show that I was calm and not at all angry, to show that, I yawned slowly, three times, very deliberately, before continuing, to make that very clear that I was not at all excited or upset.

I then stated to him as I have said that, whatever sentimental value he might attach to an old pair of shoes, surely there would be more value to his sentimental feelings, his fatherly feelings, in the act of a gift to his son. Straightforward point, a valid point.

He absolutely refused to enter into any discussion of the matter whatsoever. He quite categorically refused to answer any of the subsequent questions I put to him at that time. He simply repeated his position without discussion again and again: 'I don't want to talk about it. I don't want to talk about it.' Those were his exact words.

You can't talk to the guy. This is typical of the sort of attitude he has. This is the sort of situation you get where I am trying to put my point of view to him, to express my feelings, and he just will not listen.

So I threw a glass ornament against the wall, and the glass ornament broke as a result of that, and completely shattered into very small pieces. I also hit the door very hard with my fist to show him how I felt. What I wanted to show him was that he won't allow me to express my point of view, and that was why I did those things, to express my frustration and anger. But he just walked out of the room. And this is the sort of thing that happens.

This—this gets really heavy. My mother—my mother was standing at one end of the hallway begging me, actually literally begging me, to leave the house, to go. But he was just sitting in the lounge room pretending to read the paper. But his hand was shaking.

I was shouting at my mother. I left the door open deliberately through to the lounge so he could hear what I was saying. I was saying it to my mother, but it was really for him to hear. I said how can I communicate all these things I have to say if he won't listen? He could hear, but he would not acknowledge that he could. This is how my father conducts himself. He uses his powerful connections and his cunning to deny me my personhood. It's quite common.

Now at this time it was midsummer. My need for a pair of shoes was therefore not so urgent, so I let the matter rest. I went barefoot a lot of the time, or I would wear the kung fu shoes. I thought if he wants to refuse his son such a small thing which would do me so much good and him no harm, then he can go ahead and do it. Not my problem. Let him sweat it out.

But by the time winter was coming round I again thought that I really needed a pair of shoes. I mean, my feet, man . . .

I did go at one time into Hannah's shoe store. I looked around and I did find a pair of leather shoes which fitted me okay. They were okay. They had a good hard-wearing rubber sole with leather uppers. They would have been okay. They cost $89.95. I had the money at that time and I did almost buy them but I didn't, I don't know why, I was about to buy them but then I just walked out of the shop. I had the shoes in my hand but I dropped them to the floor. I had to get out of there. The place was very uninspiring.

So then I thought, I'll give him one more chance. One more chance to do something for his son, a small thing, a small gesture of caring between father and son, the sort of thing that should happen without even thinking.

To make sure that he did actually understand the position I was in, and the full situation, just so he couldn't say later on he didn't know all the facts or hadn't been properly informed, I made a bit of polite conversation, creating an appropriate background or backdrop. Just talking about the weather, about the condition of the roads, about the condition of my current footwear and my feet.

I then asked him again, politely and reasonably, or rather if you like I offered to him the opportunity to give me the shoes. I'd seen them there that afternoon they were still there in the wash-house. He said he would never give me his shoes. He said I should forget the whole matter, I should just forget it. He was very emphatic. He said there was absolutely no chance that he would change his mind later on, and although I offered him an opportunity just to think it over for a bit, wait till he cooled down a bit, he said no, he said his answer was final as of that moment. So I made the obvious suggestion of the logical solution, which was a fair compromise. We would share the shoes.

I would wear the shoes. If he wished to do some gardening he had only to contact me the day before, giving a clear twenty-four hours notice (and I was willing to take full responsibility for making absolutely sure that I could always be contacted at any time of the day or night), and I would immediately see to it that the shoes were returned for his use in the garden, at my own expense. Unless I was out of the country. That would be at his expense.

He told me to get out. His exact words were: 'Just get out. Just get out.'

By now I no longer had any interest in my father at all. I did not consider myself then and I don't consider myself now to be his son. I therefore proposed to him that we settle the matter once and for all: that he settle on me there and then, as his rightful heir, the benefit of any inheritance or property that would rightfully be due to me on his death, and that I in return sign or execute any document or agreement he might require or suggest as proof that he had discharged any and all obligations under that head or any other. He would then formally and legalistically disown me as his son. We would then part forever. No correspondence would be entered into, and no further claims to be pursuable at any time by either party.

I was willing to take a cheque.

I then announced my intention of leaving the country. I would go to Germany where I held the intention to seek gainful employment as a roof builder. Germany is a highly organised industrial nation with a steadily growing population. The building industry is therefore buoyant, and I had no doubt that work would be easy to find. The German people, as a nation, are highly skilled and organised. They are clean, boisterous, and they know how to get the job done, working as a team. Also they are very pure people. I felt and feel that life under these conditions would appeal to me, and that I could make a new and happy and productive life for myself in Germany.

That was on the Friday. On the Saturday morning I decided to hitch down to Wellington. I got a bus as far as Manukau City and tried to hitch a ride from there. But after two hours I still hadn't got a ride. I was feeling quite discouraged, quite low, and I decided to take a meal break as I still had $7.55 in my pocket.

After the meal break, I tried hitching again for a while, but it was starting to get dark and I still had no luck so I decided my chances of getting a ride were about nil for that night anyway. I walked back into town.

By now I was feeling very aimless, with no sense of direction, or no goal to aim for. There seemed to be nothing to pin my hopes on, in the immediate present outlook, or even for the coming days ahead. Everything had fallen through and I was frightened of the police. I began to feel very sad and depressed. Also, I had stepped in a puddle while making my way across some muddy waste ground. My feet were cold and wet.

I tried to sleep on the front steps of a church, but it was not practicable. There was a cold wind and dead leaves were blowing around. I could not prevent the dead leaves from blowing against my face in a repulsive fashion.

It seemed a very meaningless way to carry on an existence.

So I decided to return to my father's house and ask my father if he had considered my proposition. I had nowhere else to go.

When I arrived the house was empty. I remembered that they were going sailing that weekend. I had lost my key so I couldn't get inside. But the door to the wash-house was unlocked. It didn't have a lock, in fact. I went into the wash-house, planning to rest and wait.

I turned on the light and I saw there my father's shoes. They were under the sink. I went over to them. I brushed the cobwebs off them.

And I slipped my right foot into the right shoe.

There it is. The right shoe. Feels good. Good leather shoe. And then I just slipped my left foot into the left shoe, and there it was. And there I was. They're good shoes. I had no choice. I need shoes, man. He could have given them to me, but he wouldn't. It could have been a warm and giving thing between father and son, and instead he did what he has always done, he refused to give me what I asked, what I needed, what I wanted. Want your shoes, Dad. Simple. Want your shoes.

All Day Sun

'What you got on today?'

'Nothing special . . .' Greer's voice is muffled by the padding of the table top.

'Long lunch, eh?'

'Not exactly.' He closes his eyes. Strong hands on his body. The smell of therapeutic oils. Silence. Nothing like silence, he thinks. The masseur starts on his shoulders.

'So . . . what line of work are you in?'

This question, Greer does not like. When he has to fill out official forms, he is always as creative as possible with occupation. Explorer. Psychic researcher. Oxygen Metabolist. He's done it all.

'The oldest profession of all.'

'Er . . . ?'

He lets him sweat. 'I'm a full-time carer.'

'Oh, right. Oldest profession, yeah, I suppose it is. Ha ha.'

'If you think about it.'

'Nice one. So, how many?'

'Three. Seven and five, but the five-year-olds are twins.'

'That's quite a handful.'

'And another on the way.'

The masseur whistles. 'So you sent her out to work, did ya?'

'That's right. Sent her out to work.'

The masseur laughs. 'They can bloody support us for a change, eh?'

'How about you? Kids?'

'Yeah, a girl. She's thirteen. She's a real little lady.' He walks round the head of the table. 'Yep, a real little lady. But it's not like having a daughter. We're best mates, eh. We can talk about anything. It's not like that father-daughter sort of thing at all.'

Greer shifts on the table. Bet he doesn't live with her.

'Yeah, I wish I could see more of her but she's down in Christchurch with her mum, so . . . you know.'

But Greer doesn't know, not at all. Some people have no idea, he thinks, none at all. Silence again. The masseur moves to his back. The primal pleasure of being rubbed.

'So tell me a bit about the old back.' The masseur lays a proprietorial hand on Greer's lower dorsal region.

'Well it's pretty sore. It's stiff. If I get in the wrong position, sometimes it just goes. I get stuck. I can't move. And it wakes me up at night.'

'Does this hurt?' The masseur places a thumb on one of Greer's lower vertebrae. He presses, gently.

'No . . .'

'This?' Pressing harder.

'Not especially.'

'This?' His body jerks like a fish on the bottom of a boat as a million volts shoot from the base of Greer's spine to the end of his left leg and back again.

'Mm . . . not so . . . pleasant.'

The masseur starts to work, carefully. 'Looks like you've got yourself a bit of disc trouble.'

'I see.'

'And the disc is pressing on a nerve.'

'Cunning little devil.'

'Been to the quack?'

'Don't believe in 'em.'

The masseur works for a while. When he speaks again, his tone is careful. 'This is just something for you to think about, eh . . .'

Greer waits. He's going to tell me how to run my life.

'I mean this might not be you at all, right, but I get quite a lot of guys with lower back pain who are in a situation where the traditional roles are reversed, and where they're, like, not the bread-winner.'

'Is that right?'

'Yep. When the kids come along. That's what does it.'

'Does what?'

The masseur digs deeper. Greer tenses, but there is no pain. Instead a kind of dull melancholy rises up from the pit of his stomach. It reminds him of apricots. The masseur starts to talk again. 'It's all instinct. If you think about it in terms of evolution of the species, right, it was only yesterday us guys were out there spearing mammoths, right? And that was a job for the fellas. Right? I mean, no bull, the bigger, uglier and hairier you were, the better. That's just how things were. Today, you start a family, that instinct is still there. It's telling you, get out there and bring home the bacon.'

'I thought you said mammoth.'

'Cos instinct-wise, nothing's changed. But anything elsewise, everything's changed.' The masseur starts on his legs. 'Instinct. Yeah. So. All that instinct's got to go somewhere. Right? So where does it go?'

'I have a feeling you're going to tell me.'

'Straight to your lower back.' He slaps Greer's left buttock for emphasis. 'I mean, that's just something for you to think about. I'm not saying that is definitely you.'

'Oh, that's me all right.'

'Yeah?' The masseur sounds pleased. 'Because a lot of guys find that hard to deal with.'

'That's because it is hard to deal with.'

The masseur bears down on a pressure point beside Greer's left hip. Greer feels a dull, releasing pain. Again, apricots. 'So you do get those kind of feelings from time to time?'

'What, "Go hunt a mammoth you useless bastard." That kind of thing?'

'Yeah.'

'Oh, all the time, there I am, down Lambton Quay on a Friday night, a mammoth waiting at the lights, and me without my spear . . .'

The masseur chuckles. He works at Greer's left calf. It hurts. 'You know what you have to do? If you get those thoughts coming up, you gotta jump on 'em. Knock 'em straight back down. Cos they'll stress you. They'll go straight to your back and they'll stress you every time.' The masseur works harder. It feels as if his leg is being savaged by a toothless pit bull. 'Mate, these calf muscles are tighter than a fish's arsehole.'

'Hm.'

'You know what you have to do?'

'Hm?'

'Listen to your body.' The masseur leans on his work. 'You want to know what your body is saying?'

'Hm . . . ?'

'Your body is saying, chill. Chill, man, chill.'

On the way up the hill, for no good reason, Greer is having a good rational think about bank robbery. Assuming an initial outlay of say fifty dollars for a second-hand Chinese .22, plus a few more dollars for stockings, hair dye, razors and petrol, he calculates a return on investment of maybe a hundred thousand percent. That's a very attractive proposition. Sure there are risks, but assuming adequate foresight and planning they're probably easy to overstate. After all, the majority of criminals are young men and even some of them succeed. A mature balanced individual like himself would stand every chance of success in a properly conceived bank raid. Only trouble is, the way things are right now, he'd have to get the nice young man behind the desk to help him to the car. Forty years old and he's walking like an octogenarian. The massage has done him no good at all. He won't go back. He only went because he didn't dare face the doctor.

Turning to the irrational side of bank robbery, he knows exactly which bank he'd rob. He knows the branch, too, and he knows the hostage he'd take. The manager. The one who in a recent mortgage meeting addressed the first three sentences to him:

1) Sit down, sit down.

2) Coffee, or tea?

3) What exactly are your respective incomes?

Miraculously, Greer became invisible from this point on.

A yellow Rolls Royce zooms up the road. There's a young man at the wheel. Must be doing eighty kilometres an hour. Doesn't he know that children die, every day, on streets like these, up and down the country, because young men like him drive too fast? Hurt my children, I kill you. Now there's an instinct. Young men . . .

He puts a foot wrong, and pain stabs his buttock. There's something seductive about it, all this pain.

He hates young men. They're out of control. They have no sense of responsibility, fear or mortality. Young men ride their skateboards on the road and their mountain bikes on the footpath. They run, full tilt, through shopping malls. They laugh too loud. They drink beer during the day. Late teens to late twenties, they're the ones. Like that terrible, irresponsible TV ad. The one where they're playing soccer and they charge through a child's sand castle. Sylvia said they were the Brazilian national soccer squad, but that just made it worse. The message was that it's cool to kick the sand castles of innocent children. Well it isn't cool.

He checks his watch. Two-twenty. Almost time to pick up the children. He's got three days' worth of washing in the basket, dishes from last night and this morning, the place hasn't been vacuumed for a fortnight and the dog's been crapping in the polyanthus again. While he is looking at his watch, the gradient of the hill changes abruptly. He staggers, there's another agonising jolt through his lower back and down his left leg.

'Jesus!' he exclaims aloud. He can't move. His upper body is inclined at an angle of about thirty degrees. He can't straighten up and he can't bend down. Nor, however, can he stay where he is. It's a kind of paradox. He wants to giggle. His legs give way and he starts to fall, but just manages to get a hand out to a nearby wall. He leans against the wall, easing his back slowly, slowly. When he thinks he's ready to walk again he sets off at an old man's pace, every step a controlled, under-ambitious act. He shakes his head. Forty years old. Sixty's going to be a blast.

He stops at the corner and looks back at the city, spread out in front of him, white in the sun, cradled between the hills. So many houses.

He walks on.

A few doors along is a newly completed block of townhouses. Next door, in the eternal shadow of the new block, is his own modest bungalow. Double-parked on the street outside the townhouses is the yellow Rolls Royce. A local motorist is easing his vehicle, with equally exaggerated care, through the narrow span of public road left available to him by the massive yellow saloon. The developer always double-parks.

The developer himself is standing on the footpath. He knows the developer, by sight. He's seen him haranguing workmen on many a morning and afternoon over the last year and a half of intermittent construction. A year and a half of banging and drilling, of trucks and radios and an incremental blocking out of the sun.

He'd be hard to miss. Overweight, but tall. Flash suits. Collar-length reddish hair with a merino crimp to it, longer at the back than the sides: a truly ghastly haircut, a neo-Elizabethan nightmare. Drooping moustache. Yam for a nose. Suspicious, lost eyes that really wish they could trust you. Navy blazer with gold buttons with anchors on (he assumes the anchors, he's never actually got that close), putty-coloured slacks, slip-on shoes, light as ballet slippers. Appears in a range of luxury cars. Mercedes, BMW, Audi—and of course the Rolls. Probably has more trouble deciding what to drive than what to wear.

Today the developer is haranguing an electrician: 'What the fuckin' hell am I supposed to fuckin' think if he's never fuckin' here when he says he will?' He spreads his bear-like arms to show his bewilderment and hurt. He looks up and down the street, wide-eyed. The electrician shrugs and scratches his neck. The developer pulls out his cell phone.

'Where the fuck have you got to?' he barks into the cell phone as Greer approaches.

The electrician goes back to his work. He's got a panel

open in the gate post, and a mass of blue and red wires spilling out like guts. The electrician checks the wires one by one with a voltage meter. He works very slowly. He's a young man too. He looks Jamaican, but he's got a tattoo on his arm of a dragon, over the legend CYMRU.

Greer picks his way with care across the broken-up, muddy, rubbish-strewn stretch of public footpath outside the units. Over the last year and a half, the developer has used the public footpath as a metaphorical lavatory. He has dumped the refuse of his construction on it, left water flowing across it for weeks on end, strung power cables across it—at neck height—stored materials on it, blocked it with concrete mixers, utility vehicles and luxury saloons, and now, when the units are complete, the signs are up and the window boxes planted, the only unfinished thing is the footpath.

Throughout the construction period, Greer has regularly phoned to complain about the footpath. The city council have been crisply, efficiently, useless. Every time he rings they put him through the same intricate and highly developed complaint logging procedure, noting the time of his call, his name, address, phone number, the details of his complaint, even giving him a special six-digit complaint identification number for ease of future reference. He is told that an inspector will go immediately to the site, to determine what action is necessary, and that he will be informed of the outcome. Nothing has ever happened.

At the gate to his once pleasant little bit of front garden, he stops and looks back. 'When are you going to do something about this footpath?' But the developer hasn't heard him. He's arguing on the phone. The electrician is watching, though, as Greer takes a step towards the developer. The developer, still talking on his cell phone, gets into his car and zooms off, still talking. The electrician gives Greer a half-smile, and shrugs.

'Don't worry about him, man, he's just a cunt.'

*

That night, the Commonwealth Games are on TV. The children are in bed, the dog is snoring in the corner. Sylvia is exhausted. Greer is exhausted, and in a huff. He's been in a huff all evening because Sylvia was late for dinner and she didn't phone. She came in with a hang-dog expression and a story about a last minute call from head office and a computer crash, which only irritated him all the more because it sounded important and exciting.

'Why didn't you phone?'

'I'm sorry, I forgot.'

'You don't care. You just don't care.'

'I do, I do care. I just forgot. God, I'm sorry, I'm sorry.'

'If you really cared, you wouldn't forget.'

'Everything happened at once, I didn't get a chance. I'm sorry.'

'For a ten-second phone call? The dinner's ruined.'

'I'm sorry.'

'Stop saying you're sorry.'

Running over it now in his mind, he is astonished. Where does he get this stuff from? There he was in the hall, clutching a teatowel, hands on hips. If you really cared, you wouldn't forget. Incredible.

After that the huff set in, and things went smoothly if silently. The children were bathed, brushed and bedded. The dog was tripped over (by Greer), kicked (by Greer), petted (Sylvia), fed (Greer) and kicked (Greer again). The dinner was eaten in silence.

Now, the Commonwealth Games is on TV, and Greer's huff is close to expiring. A huff has a limited shelf life, and he is keenly aware that if he exceeds it he will provoke a counter-huff of even greater severity.

The 4 x 100 women's relay is about to begin. The shining young women saunter to the starting line, shaking their legs and arms.

He reads the signs: Sylvia pouring a glass of water without offering him one. Sylvia getting out some papers without comment. Sylvia doing some work without apology. Greer has an uncomfortable feeling that he's already left it too late. There's nothing worse than the moment when you realise that you've overplayed your huff. Easy to do of course; huffmanship is a complex and subtle sport, demanding concentration, stamina and determination.

The runners are crouched on their blocks, their bodies taut.

'If men are the sport-watchers of the nation, I cannot for the life of me understand why women's athletics is not the most popular sport on television.'

Nothing. Not a flicker.

He sighs and looks across at her. She's doing her tax return. He knows what the big figure is. Total taxable income. He did his own return earlier in the month. Took him ten minutes.

The starter's pistol cracks.

The IRD is the one institution with whom he resists the temptation to be creative about his job description. Housewife, is what he puts. Housewife, followed by a string of zeroes. That pretty much sums it up.

He yawns, ostentatiously. 'God, I'm shagged.'

It might as well be the sphinx sitting next to him, doing her tax return.

The young women are flying, their toes barely touching the ground.

Greer sniffs, wrinkles his nose. 'Jesus, that dog needs a bath.'

Cold silence.

There is a roar from the television as a shining young woman, her bright blond hair flapping madly like a banner, bursts through the tape just ahead of several other shining young women. The four members of the winning team embrace, tears of joy in their eyes.

'Any chance of a refund then?'

'Fuck off.'

A breakthrough. But be careful, mustn't be too chatty, he'll only come across as desperate. He yawns again, gets up and goes to the kitchen. His back is hurting. The kitchen is a mess. He actually caught up, briefly, today, about four-fifteen in the afternoon, just after he finally got last night's put away and before he had to start on dinner for the kids. He still remembers that moment of purity, the bench clean and white, stretching away from him like a prairie.

Careful to make just enough noise so she'll hear it in the lounge, but not enough so she'll think he's doing it on purpose, he clatters the dishes as he tidies.

'How's the back?' Guarded tone, flat delivery. She comes up behind him, pours another glass of water. Careful now.

'Oh, can't complain.' He turns and smiles bravely. Bravery is becoming a salient feature of domestic life. Sylvia is brave about working far too hard for a woman in her condition; Greer is brave about his lack of prospects and his back. 'Feeling sick?'

'Not particularly.' She smiles bravely, and picks up a teatowel. She sighs heavily. 'God I'm tired.'

'Oh don't.' He regrets it the moment he's said it.

'Don't what?'

'There's nothing more tiring than talking about how tired you are.'

'I bloody am tired.'

'So bloody am I. That's my point.' Damn. Damn damn damn. 'Listen, kid, I know you're tired, hell, I'm tired myself, if we weren't tired we wouldn't be human.'

She hits him with the tea towel.

'Hey.'

She hits him again.

'What's that for?'

'For being so bloody grumpy all the time.'

'I wasn't being grumpy, I was being amusing.'

She shakes her head.

The dishes are done. It's now ten-thirty. They're shagged, fucked, utterly exhausted. His back is burning. Her stomach is queasy. His leg aches. Her vision is blurred. All they can think of is bed. And now, to work.

'What about this? Four bedrooms, secluded bush setting.'

'Forget it.' Sylvia turns a page aggressively.

'What's wrong with it?'

'No sun.'

'But it doesn't say anything about sun.'

'Exactly. Unless it specifically says "all-day sun" or at least "sun-drenched" it's as dark as the pit of hell.'

'Okay what about this then—"sun-drenched site, drive-on access, family living at its best, range three-fifty–four-fifty".'

'How many bedrooms?'

'Five. And a double garage, and a study.'

She looks across the table. 'What's wrong with it?'

'Nothing.'

'Where is it?'

'Not far.'

'Where?'

'Upper Hutt.'

She rolls her eyes. He's always trying this one on. 'I'm not living in Upper Hutt.'

'Might be nice. Move out to the suburbs, get a horse . . .'

'And drive forty minutes to work. Forget it.'

'Some people commute two hours a day.'

'Some people are stupid.'

'The children would love it.'

'I am not going to live in Upper Hutt. Face it. Why do you think it's so cheap out there?'

He's gone back to the paper. 'Hey, wait a second, look look look. Now this is a serious proposition. Northland, four bedrooms, spa—nice touch—drive-on access . . .'

She's leaning over his shoulder. 'We've been there. Number forty-four. The one with the holes in the ceiling. Remember?'

He looks again. 'Cunning bastards, they've changed the picture.'

By eleven-fifteen they've been through the property sections in both papers. They've ringed half-a-dozen possibles. Greer will make the calls tomorrow.

By midnight, they're in bed.

'Sex.'

'Yer what?'

'You know. Sex.'

'Oh, that.'

'Yeah, that.'

'I remember that. We used to do that, didn't we?'

'Like rabbits.'

'That's right. It was quite fun, wasn't it?'

'Mm-hm. Quite.'

'Lights out?'

'Lights out.'

'Good night, dear.'

'Sleep well and all that.'

Silence. Purple blotches in front of his eyes. His left foot is tingling. 'I saw the bastard today.'

'How was he?'

'Fucking disgusting. A haircut to die of.'

'Was he in the Mercedes?'

'The Rolls.'

'The yellow one?'

'There is only one Rolls, sweetheart.' Condescending.

'I thought there were two.'

'Not Rollses, BMWs. There are two BMWs. A yellow and

a green. A 318i and a 740L. The 318 is the yellow one. It's got spoilers. The 740 hasn't.' He shifts, gets a jolt, and grimaces in the dark. The purple blotches explode, scatter and regroup. 'Remind me to phone the council tomorrow.'

'I thought they never did anything.'

'That's exactly what I'm going to tell them.'

She plumps her pillow, and puts a hand on his arm. 'Do you want the good news or the bad news?'

He knows perfectly well there won't be any good news. 'Oh, the good news, by all means.'

'I did get a refund on my tax return.'

'How much?'

'Four dollars.'

'Four dollars? Well, why didn't you say so? Now we can buy that Roseneath residence with en-suite swimming pools and turbo bum-cleaner.'

His hip is already beginning to ache. He wonders how long he will sleep tonight. He's been sleeping on his front the last couple of days because lying on his back hurts too much. As for lying on his side, the only position in which he finds it possible actually to sleep, that's been out for the last week. He tries to find a more comfortable position. No dice. 'What's the bad news?'

'I have to go to Auckland next week.'

'Fuck.'

'All-day meeting.'

Be brave. 'When?'

'Tuesday.'

'What flight?'

'The red-eye.'

'Holy Jesus, Mother of God.'

'Thought I was the lapsed Catholic in this house.'

'Beg your absolution.'

'Granted.'

He sighs. 'When do you get back?'

'Nine. And it's Holy Mary, Mother of God.'

'What did I say?'

'Holy Jesus.'

'Holy Jesus, Mother of God?'

''Fraid so.'

'I'm losing it. Holy Jesus.'

'Mother of God.'

'Night.'

'Night.'

He shifts to get comfortable, but it only hurts the more. He groans.

'Was that you groaning?'

'Either that or we've got company.'

'I feel sick.'

'Why are we doing this?'

'Doing what?'

'Whatever we're doing.'

'What choice do we have?'

'Oblivion.'

'Nope, can't do that. We've got children.'

'Let's face it. We're husks of our former selves. We're tired, depressed, our lives are meaningless, and our bodies don't work. And from here on it only gets worse.'

'If only we could find a house that we actually like, and is big enough for a family of four children, and we can actually afford.'

'For Chrissake, this is ridiculous. If people like us can't afford suitable houses, who can? We're middle class. We've got it easy.'

'Easy?'

'We can't complain can we?'

'Middle-class complaining is traditionally frowned upon.'

'And with good reason. I mean, God, once you've got the

middle class complaining, you know what you've got.'

'What?'

'Revolution, that's what.'

'Oh, yeah.'

'G'night.'

She reaches out again. He feels her hand on his shoulder. 'Will you still love me when I'm old and decrepit?'

'Not a chance.' She punches his arm. 'Anyway, by the time you're old and decrepit I'll be old and dead.'

'How do you know?'

'Men always die first.'

'Not always.'

'Usually.'

'How's your blood pressure?'

'Dunno.'

'Weren't you supposed to go to the doctor?'

'I'm not going to see that bastard.'

'Why not?'

'Because he's going to put me on pills next time I see him, that's why.'

'Really?'

'Beta-blockers.'

'For your blood pressure?'

'Yeah. They calm you down too.'

'You won't know yourself.'

'You know what the side-effects are?'

'What?'

'Loss of libido.'

They laugh, hollowly.

'That's something to do with sex isn't it?'

'Sex?'

'Yeah, you know. That thing.'

'Oh, that.'

*

He wakes at two a.m., on the dot. His hip is on fire. He suppresses a groan, and rolls out of bed. His back is so stiff he can't reach to put shoes on, but he slips on a dressing gown. He goes into the hall. If he can walk it off, maybe he'll get some sleep. He paces the hall for a bit, until Sylvia calls from the bedroom: 'Can you not groan quite so loud, please?'

'Sorry,' he calls back, 'I'm just in fucking agony out here.' But there's no answer. He sighs. He's going to have to go outside. He limps to the kitchen and takes too many Disprin.

The moonlight is pouring down, saturating everything. The grass is white-blue. Cool between his toes. The stars are visible on the horizon, but for the rest of it, it's just this huge cold fish of a moon. He wonders if it's gibbous. He suspects it might be. He begins to pace. Up and down, up and down, from the fence to the hedge and back again. Every now and again he throws in a moan. He works out a routine. He does a single moan in the middle of the garden, and a double moan at each end of the beat. He looks up at the moon. He moans. He's moaning at the moon. 'Things can't go on like this,' he says, aloud, to the moon. The moon shines down.

A half hour later the Disprin is taking just enough of the edge off. He can cut the moaning. He goes back to bed, eases himself in beside his sleeping, exhausted, pregnant, hard-working, very slightly snoring wife, and stares at the moon on the curtains. At some point he begins a fitful doze, but not a single one of the hours on the glowing face of the digital radio alarm escape him: three o'clock, four o'clock, five o'clock, he greets each one.

The alarm rings at six. Sylvia moans and gets out of bed. He tries to roll out of bed too and succeeds, but when he tries to stand he has to lean on the bedside table with all his weight to get into a position even approximating vertical.

Sylvia's in the shower as he lurches to the kitchen, bracing himself on walls and in doorways. The children are still in bed. He decides to make lunches, fumbles in the cupboard, working with one supporting hand on the bench-top. His torso has skewed off to one side, and his back feels like concrete. He gets the bread on the bench, and the makings, but one-handed spreading of peanut butter sandwiches is an impossibility. He ends up waving the slice of bread on the end of the knife, like a flag of surrender. He shifts his weight, curses as the pain surges, gasps, puts both hands on the bench and carefully slips down the wall to the floor. He crawls back to the bedroom, hauls himself onto the bed and lies face down, breathing shallowly. Sylvia comes back from the shower.

'Where's my bra?'

'Do you think you could you get my jeans started?' Unable to reach his knees, let alone his feet, he'll have to rely on charity to get dressed this morning. Sylvia slips yesterday's jeans over his feet and jerks them up to his thighs. He groans, and works them up the rest of the way. He isn't even going to think about showering. 'Socks?' Swiftly, Sylvia finds him some socks, puts them on, and follows up with a pair of sneakers. She kneels and laces them for him. She strides about the room, frantic.

'God, I'm so tired.' She vanishes.

There's a crash, a thump and a squeal. His body tenses involuntarily, and his ears prick up like an old dog at the hunting horn. Instinct. He should be there in the kitchen. He's always there. There's a crash as something biggish bounds into the room. He's too exhausted to turn his head to see. It's either Nathan or the dog. A wettish snuffling in his ear. Nathan.

'Mum says are you going to make the lunches.'

'Tell Mum sorry but I can't move.'

Nathan bounds out. Greer decides he'd better try to get up. He puts a hand on the bed and tries to roll over, but it just hurts too much. Everything hurts.

Nathan's back. 'Mum says did you do any underpants for me?'

'In the dryer.'

Crash. He's gone. He can hear his ear-shattering soprano in the kitchen: 'Dad says they're in the dryer.'

An inaudible murmur. Crash. Nathan's back. 'Mum says did you iron her shirts yesterday like you promised.'

'Shit.'

Crash. In the kitchen: 'Dad says shit.'

'No!' calls Greer, 'I didn't say shit!' No response. 'Fuck!' Gritting his teeth, he forces himself onto the floor, on his knees. He crawls to the kitchen doorway and climbs up the wall and onto his feet. He stands in the doorway, leaning heavily on the door frame, sweat beading his brow. 'Sorry,' he gasps.

She's doing the sandwiches in her bra. Nathan's eating toast, wearing his underpants on his head. Katie's eating prunes, and her twin, Bella, is running round the room making aeroplane noises. The dog watches Katie eat her prunes, from bowl to mouth and back to bowl, like a tennis match. 'I'll wear yesterday's.'

'They won't eat that jam. They don't like it.'

Sylvia looks up from the sandwiches. She compresses her lips.

'Well they don't.'

'Too late now.' She drops the sandwiches in the boxes. He decides to say nothing about the raisins. 'I have to go. I'll have to get a taxi, I'm going to be late. Will you be all right to drive them?'

'Yep.' He pushes off from the door jamb to demonstrate and almost faints, but Sylvia hasn't noticed. She grabs her briefcase, kisses the nearest child, pecks him on the cheek, and is gone.

He takes stock. He has to get the kids to school. He has to get down the path and into the car. 'Nathan, come here.' Nathan bounds over. 'I want you to listen very carefully. Nathan, take your underpants off your head.'

'Why?'

'I can't talk to a boy with his underpants on his head.'

'Why not?'

'What in God's name have you got on under your trousers anyway?'

'They're not trousers, they're shorts.'

'What's under them?'

Nathan thinks. 'Nothing,' he says, brightly.

Katie is giving her prunes to the dog. 'Katie! Stop that! The dog's going to be inside all day.'

He turns back to his son. 'Listen. I need you to help me, Nathan. Can you do that?'

'Sure.'

'I need you to put your underpants where they're supposed to be. Then, I need you to help me get these two into the car.'

'Easy-peasy.' Nathan turns to the nearest twin, grabs her by the ear and begins to drag her, squealing like a stuck pig, towards the front door.

'Nicely, Nathan, nicely!'

Nathan rolls his eyes.

'And let's start with the underpants.'

They make it to school, somehow, only twenty minutes late. After the kids have gone he forces himself to walk up and down the footpath, trying to get his back into some sort of working order. If he can just get it going, he'll be all right. Late morning, early afternoon are his best times. After five or ten minutes he's managed to correct the sideways skew, and he's beginning to feel a little better.

When he gets home he parks outside the front gate. In order to get out of a car, it is generally necessary to duck one's head by about five or six inches. But this, he cannot do. If he tries to duck his head, a sharp tingling starts at the top of his buttocks. By the time his head has travelled two inches the sharp tingling has become an intense jabbing pain. From here the pain increases logarithmically. He sits for a few moments, sweating with frustration. He can see the electrician from yesterday, still working on the front gate of the units next door. He hesitates, then blows the horn. The electrician glances up, looks around, then goes back to his work. He blows the horn again. The electrician looks up again, sees Greer this time. Greer waves him over. The electrician waves back, and goes on with his work. Greer blows the horn again, and waves more urgently. The electrician puts down his screwdriver and saunters over, looking cautious.

'Can I help you, man?'

'I'm sorry but I wonder if you could move my leg for me.'

It takes them almost five minutes to manoeuvre him onto the footpath and over to the electrician's gatepost, where Greer leans, panting.

'Are you going to be all right man?'

'Yes, yes, I'm fine, it's just getting started. I'll rest here for a minute then I'll be right as rain.'

'Well all right, man.' The electrician doesn't look convinced, but he takes up the screwdriver again. Greer watches. He's always admired the skill of an honest tradesman.

'What are you doing?'

'Fixing this fucking gate, man.'

'What's wrong with it?'

'Doesn't fucking work, does it?'

He can't tell if he sounds Jamaican or Welsh. 'Where's the boss?'

'How would I know?'

'How do you put up with him?'

'He's just a cunt, man, you get used to them in my line of business. He's just a spoilt child. Believe me, I should know man.' Probably Jamaican, thinks Greer.

'Got kids yourself?'

'No man, but I'm a spoilt fucking child myself. Takes one to know one, man.'

'I've got three.'

'For God's sake, man, tie a fucking knot in it before it's too late.' On the other hand, could be Welsh.

'It is too late.'

The electrician shakes his head. 'What a bloody tragedy.'

Greer laughs, and a stab of pain travels up one leg. He leans more heavily on the gatepost. 'Don't you want kids?'

'Can't afford them, man. The wife, she wants kids, but I say to her, no fucking way, you stay at work until the fucking van's paid off and we have a fucking deposit on a fucking house. I'm not bringing up kids in rental fucking accommodation.' No, must be Jamaican.

'But you do want kids?'

'I'm resigned to the inevitable, man.'

'What's your wife do?'

'She's a receptionist but she goes to night school. She works fucking hard she does and a fucking bloody brain box she is too. She works harder than me. I don't know how she does it. I get home every night and I switch on the television. Put my feet up and drink a beer. Or else I'm down the pub. But my wife, she gets home and she hits the fucking books.' Welsh-Jamaican?

'Good for her.'

'And in bed, great God almighty in heaven, I can't tell you. She's a real woman all right.' Welsh, definitely.

'Been married long?'

'Six weeks, man.' The electrician sighs. 'I tell you this for free, man, if women were running the fucking world today we wouldn't be in the bloody fucking mess we're in, man.'

'Aren't they?'

'Aren't they what?'

'Running the world?'

'No, it's a man's fucking world all right.'

'How do you figure that?'

'Just look at the bloody fucking mess we're in, man. That's man's work, man. No woman would do that, man.'

There's a subdued eight-cylinder murmur behind them. Without turning around he knows it's the Rolls. The developer comes across to the gate, ignoring Greer.

'Gonna get that finished this arvo?'

The electrician shrugs. 'Depends.'

'On what?'

Greer feels solidarity. He wants to say something devastating but he can't think of anything. The developer looks at Greer, up and down. Greer notices he has been parked in. They eye each other like knife fighters.

'Are people actually buying these things?' It was supposed to be caustic and cutting but it came out peevish.

The developer looks away, down the street. All Greer can see is the back of his head. 'Yeah, they're moving.'

'How many have you sold?'

The developer squints at the sky, then back down the street. 'Got one away. We'll the flick the rest on.'

'It's taken you long enough.'

'First guy went belly-up. Council changed the rules on him.' His tone is matter-of-fact. The developer dials a number on his cell phone. He lifts it to his mouth.

'Sort of a Mediterranean look,' says Greer, loudly, unwilling to be dismissed. The developer glances at Greer, then up at the building behind him. There's a huge sign across the front: MEDITERRANEAN LIFE-STYLE UNITS. He turns away and presses the phone to his ear.

'So when are you going to clean up the footpath?'

The developer looks away from Greer, down the street, way, way down the street. He starts to mutter into his cell phone.

'I'm going to need my car in a while,' says Greer, easing his weight off the gatepost. He's skewed off to the side again, but he can walk.

There are six answerphone messages, all from real estate agents. He works through them, standing at the table in the hall, noting phone numbers, addresses, numbers of bedrooms. Then he starts ringing back.

'Greer, how are you?'

'Graham, great, thanks. Fury Crescent . . . ?'

'I think this really could work for you. It's a lovely, tidy little—'

'Is it sun-drenched?'

'Sorry?'

'Is it drenched in sun?'

'Oh, sure, it gets sun.'

'But is it drenched?'

'Drenched?'

'Has to be drenched.'

'I'd say more . . . sunny and sheltered.'

'Appreciate your honesty.'

He makes one appointment, for midday. Then he rings Sylvia: 'I've got a possible at twelve.'

'Sorry I can't today.'

'I'll have a look and tell you about it.'

He puts on a load of washing, hooking the clothing items one at a time out of the basket, with a straightened-out wire coat hanger. He eats a couple of bananas and starts to feel better. When he comes down to the street at twenty past eleven, he's walking more or less smoothly. He thinks he might be able to get back into the car.

He's still parked in. There's no sign of the developer. He goes over to the electrician.

'Upstairs.' The electrician points with his screwdriver.

*

It's a top-floor flat, three bedrooms. Light floods into the west-facing windows. The smell of new paint, the thickness of new carpet, but the room is the size of a cupboard. It's crap housing and in ten years it'll be a slum. There's no sign of the developer. Greer goes to the windows. It's a fantastic day, sunny and clear. To his left the view opens out right across the city to the brooding varicose hills on the far side. To his right is a glittering slice of the inner harbour. This is his view. He'd recognise it anywhere. He used to stand at his front door and watch this view change with the seasons and the times of day. Now he stands at his front door and enjoys the back of the townhouses. He can see the Rolls in the street, parking him in.

There's a loud cough behind him. 'Can I help you, mate?' The developer has come from the bedrooms. He puts his hands on his hips.

'I asked you to move your car.'

'What's the problem?'

'You've parked me in, that's the problem.'

The developer turns around, reaching for his keys. Greer can't help himself. 'When are you going to fix that bloody footpath?'

There's no mistaking the belligerence of his tone. The developer stops, his small eyes shimmying. 'When the fuckin' builder comes round and finishes the fuckin' job, that's when.'

'And when's that going to be?'

The developer shrugs, spreads his arms wide. 'Ask him.'

'I'm asking you.'

The developer shakes his head, turns around and goes down the stairs.

'It's your responsibility!' Greer is almost shouting, but the rounded, bearish shoulders have disappeared downstairs. Incensed, Greer follows. He comes out into bright sunshine, and is momentarily blinded. The developer is already reversing his car.

The electrician sings under his breath: 'He's a cunt, he's a cunt, he's a cunt, yeah yeah yeah yeah, he's a cunt he's a cunt, yeah yeah he's cunt, he's cunt, he won't change any mo-ore . . .' He grins and winks. Jamaican, no question.

Greer looks at his watch. Eleven forty-five. He's going to be late now.

Greer is standing on a buffalo-grass lawn. At his feet a bush clad hillside plunges dramatically all the way to the gleaming surface of the city reservoir. Beyond the reservoir is the city itself, shining and distant, fading into the shimmering blue harbour. Above and beyond, above the haze, are the mountains. They'll be snow-capped in winter. Greer stands and inhales the view. Beside him, old-fashioned roses are arranged in beds. Bees are humming. The sweet smell of honeysuckle flows up the bank.

Behind him is a wide, level lawn, perfect for cricket, for romping and rolling, bordered by graceful shade trees. Behind the lawn is a quaint three-bedroom cottage. Tatty, to be sure, but loveably so. Short a bedroom, yes, but there's room to build.

He looks around. There isn't another house in sight. And as for the sky; up here the sky is as wide as the day is long. And how long is the day? It's as long as the sun is in the sky. And as for the sun; drenched doesn't begin to describe it. This is the real thing. This is sun as God intended it: true, full, unabbreviated sunshine from arsehole to breakfast, from breakfast to dinner, from sunrise to sunset. Whatever the South Pacific gets, this site gets it too. *This* is All Day Sun. Greer is dizzy with joy. He has completely forgotten his back.

'Nice little spot, eh?' There's a young man in a shiny suit leaning on the woodpile, but Greer doesn't care, he loves all life forms equally. He turns to him, his eyes shining. 'I need to call my wife.' The young man holds out a cell phone. Greer dials.

'I've found it.'

'My shirt?'

'Our house. I've found it. It's fantastic. It's got roses.'

'How many bedrooms?'

'Don't worry about all that, I'm coming to get you now.'

'I'm in a meeting.'

'Get out of it.'

'I can't.'

'You have to. I'm serious.'

'Are you sure?'

'I'm sure.'

He arranges to meet the agent back here in forty minutes, walks almost briskly to the car.

He drives as fast as he can. Sylvia is waiting on the street. He babbles all the way back. At first she is infected by his enthusiasm, but as the road winds up out of the city and into the hills, she falls silent.

He drives right up to the front door. Gingerly, he clambers out. 'Come and see the view.' But she has already gone into the house. He follows.

She's standing in the hall. She can't bring herself to look at him, and her voice is low, controlled. 'There are only three bedrooms.'

'I know, I know, but we could easily build onto the kitchen.'

'Who wants a bedroom off the kitchen?'

'So we'll move the kitchen.'

She steps into the kitchen and looks around.

'They sure built 'em to last back then,' says the agent.

'We couldn't possibly afford to do what has to be done here.'

'Yes we could.'

'No we couldn't.'

'If we get it for three-fifty.'

'They're asking four and a half.'

'If we cut a few corners.'

He can't keep the pleading out of his voice. 'Come and look at the garden. Just come and see.'

She follows him to the garden. He turns to her with his arms outspread. 'Look at it,' he says. 'Look at it.'

She nods but her face is dead. 'Very nice.'

'It's all day sun.'

Sylvia looks at him. She ticks off on her fingers. 'The house is too small and it's a mess. It's dark, damp and needs major repair. It's twenty minutes drive to the city in good traffic. I grant you the garden is nice . . .'

'And the sun.'

'The sun is good.'

'No. It's perfect. Perfect.'

'All right, the sun is perfect. But everything else is completely wrong. And who's going to look after a garden like this?

'I am.'

'With your back?'

All the way back to town, Greer is trying to think of a reason why he should be married to this woman. He can think of three. He has to pick them up in an hour.

Dropping her off, he speaks flatly. 'I don't want you to go to Auckland next week. I'm in constant back pain and I can't manage.'

She turns on him. 'You resent my job, don't you?'

'I resent being taken for granted.'

'I resent being made to feel guilty for having to work.'

'Well I resent . . .' He trails off. What exactly does he resent?

'If you don't like it, get a job yourself.'

As she gets out, she turns to him. 'I'm going to be in a

meeting for the rest of the afternoon, trying to make up for the time I've wasted today. I'm going to leave my secretary instructions not to pass on any calls. Including you.' She slams the door, and storms into the building. He revs the engine as he goes.

The developer is leaning on his Rolls Royce, dialling a number on his cell phone. There is a man in green overalls scrubbing the window boxes under the ground-floor windows of the units. Water is running across the broken-up footpath, reducing it to a quagmire. Greer recognises the hose he's using. It's his hose. It's connected to his tap, just inside the gate, on his property.

He gets out of the car. He walks towards the developer. He can't see clearly through a thin red haze. As he passes the gatepost, he trips on a piece of four-by-two lying on the torn-up surface of the footpath. He gives a shout, and catapults forward, landing on his hands and knees. He whimpers, topples slowly onto his side, and lies in the mud, gasping like a fish out of water. The electrician hurries over.

'Are you all right, man?' He looks scared.

The developer comes over too, but stays at a distance. Greer is having trouble breathing. 'This is your doing.' He gasps at the developer. 'This is your fault. I've complained a hundred times about this footpath and no one's done a thing. I'll sue, I'll sue.' He begins to weep.

The electrician looks at the developer. The developer looks at the man in green overalls, who looks at the electrician.

'Shall I call an ambulance?' says the developer.

'Do you want an ambulance, man?' The electrician bends down to Greer.

'No,' says Greer. He lies still. He sighs.

'Do you think you can get up, man?' says the electrician.

Greer makes a tentative move of his head, but collapses,

gasping. He giggles, then falls silent. He notices the sky behind the electrician's head. He's all right, this electrician. He's a young man, but he's all right.

'Well, what do you want to do, man?'

'Is he all right?' asks the developer, again. Greer can see the apprehension in his face. You're worried now, you bastard. Greer concentrates fiercely on the electrician.

'Tell him to—' He breaks off.

'What is it, man?'

'What's the time?'

'Ten to three, man.'

'My kids. I have to pick up my kids at three.'

'Isn't there someone we can phone for you, man?'

Sylvia's face flashes before his eyes. 'No. There's no one.' The electrician looks up at the developer. The developer looks at the man in green overalls. The man in green overalls looks at the developer. The developer looks up the street.

'So what do you want to do?'

'Just get me to my car.'

The electrician shakes his head. 'I don't think you should be driving, man.'

'I have to pick up my children.'

The developer looks down the street. There is no one coming to his assistance. 'All right, all right. I'll go and pick up the kids. What do they look like?'

But Greer shakes his head. 'They'd never accept a lift from a stranger. You'll have to take me.'

Acting under Greer's instructions, moving very slowly, the two men help Greer into the car. He lies across the back seat. The leather is yellow, and soft as a baby's skin against his cheek. The whole car smells new. He closes his eyes and hears the heavy thunk of the driver's door swinging shut.

'Where to?' The developer's voice is full of controlled aggravation.

Greer names the school. 'And make it quick. I have to be there in five minutes.'

'Jesus Christ, they'll wait for you, won't they?'

'I'm never late.' The developer mutters something, the car surges forward, and Greer falls silent. Pins and needles shoot up and down his leg, and his left buttock and lower back throb mercilessly. They drive.

'Where are we?'

'Cambridge Terrace.'

'Jesus, I thought we'd be halfway up Dixon Street by now.'

'It always seems longer if you can't see where you're going.'

They drive. The engine sounds like an animal. Greer casts about in his mind for the right animal.

'We're turning right into The Terrace.' The developer's words are born out by a sharp right turn that presses Greer's feet into the opposite door. His spine explodes in all directions. Molten shards pierce liver, kidneys, spleen and lungs.

Greer moans.

'You right, mate?' Even the developer sounds concerned.

'Yes, yes, yes, drive, drive,' Greer snaps, but the developer sneaks a look over this shoulder. His moustache droops in alarm.

'Jesus, you look fucked.'

'Just drive the fucking car!' he shrieks. Reason has left the building. The developer drives. Greer presses his face into the seat, his fingers digging into the leather. Time stops. Finally, the deep roar of the beast drops to a subdued murmur.

'Here we are,' says the developer. He leans over the seat and his face is almost tender. 'You still with us?'

'Open the door.'

The developer gets out and opens the door. If he raises his head, Greer can now see across the road to the school gate. They're there, standing by the gate, looking around. Nathan is balancing on a wall and the twins are watching him. Katie turns for a moment, and looks across the road. She's looking right at him, but she doesn't see. 'Katie,' calls Greer, feebly, but it's like one of those dreams where you call and call but nobody can hear you. She looks around, a vague, worried expression on her face. He calls again, but there's no strength in his lungs.

The developer crosses the road, and Greer watches as he goes up to the kids. Nathan, teetering on the wall, bends down to listen and Bella edges closer, to take Katie's hand. Instinctively, the three children step back. Greer wants to cheer. The developer steps back too, and turns and points across the road at Greer. The children look guardedly in his direction as he waves weakly from the back seat. Looks turn to surprise, then relief, and excitement. Nathan jumps down from the wall and starts to gallop across the road. 'Look right and left!' Greer bellows, hoarsely, but the developer can move faster than you might think. He has all three in line and marches them across, four abreast.

'Why are you lying down, Dad?'

'Who's he, Dad?'

'Is this our car, Dad?'

'It's really *cool*.'

'Can we go for a drive?'

'Is *he* coming?'

'Can I sit in the front?'

Katie is quiet, looking uncertainly at Greer's pale, pain-ravaged features. A brief silence falls.

'Are you okay, Dad?'

'I'm fine, sweetheart, I've just got a bit of a sore back.'

Nathan looks uncertain. 'Where's Mum?'

'Mum's busy.'

The developer steps in. 'You kids get in and we'll get you home.'

But Greer holds up a hand. 'Seat belts.'

The developer shrugs impatiently. 'What about them?'

'They must have seat belts.'

'That's going to be a bit hard with you sprawled across the back seat, isn't it, mate?'

'They have to be strapped in.'

'Look, I'll drive slowly, okay?'

'No exceptions. Children must be strapped in.'

'So what do we do?'

Greer braces himself.

'I can just crouch down here, Dad,' says Nathan, crouching behind the driver's seat.

'Yeah, me too,' says Katie, jumping in to join him. But Greer shakes his head.

'Must . . . wear seat belts. Always.' He realises he's beginning to talk like a radio play. He scrabbles feebly at the back of the seat, hooks a finger in the edge of a built-in ashtray, and pulls. The ashtray comes out and he is dusted with fine cigar ash. The developer curses.

'Get me out.'

'What are you talking about?' The developer is alarmed.

'I'm sitting in the front.'

'You can't sit in the front like that.'

'My children will wear seat belts.'

Inching himself, feet first, out the open passenger door, Greer gets himself onto the footpath, and the developer helps him into the front passenger seat. As he settles into the plush leather, he hears rather than feels a billion-volt surge straight to the brain.

When he comes round he's still in the seat, but the pain is so intense he's astonished. It soars like a sea bird, rising, rising, and he is carried on it, forever moving, up and up, higher and higher. Pain replaces time as the medium of lived experience.

Sound floods suddenly into his ears. 'Dad?'

The developer is ringing an ambulance.

Bella is telling Katie not to worry. Katie is telling Bella not to worry.

Nathan is calling him: 'Dad? Dad?' He wants to answer, but he can't quite catch his breath.

I'll die before you. When did he say that? To whom did he say that?

Bella is crying. Katie is crying. Nathan is crying. The developer leans down close to Greer's face and tells him an ambulance is on the way.

'Thank you,' he tries to say it. He tries to keep utterly still, concentrating only on this: he is waiting for an ambulance. If he waits for an ambulance, an ambulance will come. This is all he needs to know. The children are crying.

Later, the kids have stopped crying. A man in a uniform is asking Greer if he can feel this.

Feel what?

They load him into the ambulance. 'The children,' he gasps.

The developer is standing by. 'Don't worry about the kids,' he says.

They're standing in a family group as the ambulance doors close, waving goodbye. 'Seat belts,' calls Greer, feebly.

He is lying on his back in a peaceful ward. It's early evening. An unseen transistor radio is lisping in a corner, hospital dinner smells drift in from the corridor. Greer's not hungry. He's been given morphine. Surfing a particularly fierce wave, he smiles crookedly to himself as Sylvia, puffy-eyed in her business suit, wobbles towards him. She returns the smile but immediately breaks down. 'Oh God, Greer,' she brushes tears aside with the tips of her fingers. 'I thought you were dying.' She kneels at his bedside, picks up his hand and presses it to her forehead. 'I was sobbing all the way. The taxi driver thought I was nuts.'

He sighs, joyously, and concentrates on his wave. After a

while it begins to ease off. He strokes her hair.

'I'm not dying.'

'Well, the children are—to see you. I'll bring them tomorrow. I left them with Ken, just in case.'

'Who?'

'Ken. He drove you to school.'

'I never asked his name.'

'Well, it's Ken.'

'Ken . . .'

'He's such a nice guy.'

'A prince.'

'Thank God he was there when it happened. The kids adore him.'

'Do they?'

'He had them set up in one of the units. Happy Meals all round.'

'Which unit?'

'Four.'

Greer ponders. 'Harbour view?'

'Christ, I wasn't thinking about the view. I thought you were dying, Greer. I dropped in, saw the kids were okay and came straight on here. Ken said not to worry, they'll be fine. He seemed to be enjoying himself. I thought we should say thank you. I could get him a bottle of Moët on the way back. What do you think?'

'Lindauer.'

'Sweetheart . . .'

'Yes, sweetheart?' There's another wave gathering.

'I'm sorry about today. I was thinking. We could make a go of that house.'

'No.' He takes her hand. His eyes roll backwards in his head. 'Wow . . .'

She sits forward, anxious. 'What is it?'

'Nothing.' He smiles crookedly.

Sylvia smooths his hair. 'I won't go to Auckland. I had a word with them, they'll send someone else. I'm taking the week off and your mother's coming down to help with the kids.' She starts to cry again. 'Just think, if you'd died, our last words would have been words of anger.'

'Hey,' says Greer. He takes her hand. 'Chill.' And kisses it. 'Chill, man, chill.'

Rat

Perry and James had a little competition going. Every time Perry got one, it was a notch on the left side of the wooden handle of the big kitchen carving knife. Every time James got one, it was a notch on the right. So far, Perry had three notches, James had four.

Of the total, seven mice, four had been chopped, one trampled, one crushed and one bludgeoned. They had contrasting styles. Perry was the specialist—all three of his kills had been with the knife. He would squat for hours by the oven, the blade poised in his hand, waiting for a mouse to poke its nose out. That was all it took. One peek and he'd have their heads off. James's style was more eclectic, working off instinct and the inspiration of the moment. He'd be reading the paper in the lounge, or practising yoga in the hall. Suddenly, without warning, he'd bound across the room in a blur of movement, snatching up an empty beer bottle, or a fly swat, or a discarded shoe as he ran. A mouse would die.

Under the rules of play, a kill could only be claimed if the body was presented for inspection by the other party. Road-kill, cat-kill or death by natural causes were not eligible, nor was poisoning or trapping. The only legitimate kill was one resulting directly from an act of violence carried out by one of the two participants, acting alone.

The bodies were added one by one to a mass grave in the back garden. Perry was going to dig up the skulls in six months time and make earrings to sell at the market. James was collecting tails to make a belt. They'd tried to skin one but it was too fiddly.

Perry was desperate to even the score with James. Secretly envious of James's easy-going, mercurial charm, his honey-blond hair and success with girls, he wanted to prove something. He wanted to prove that cold, continent precision, as characterised by his own killing style, was superior. By sheer strength of will, he would overcome. Perry spent long hours hunched over the back of the stove, still as stone, carving knife in hand. But the mice had learnt to keep away, and Perry waited in vain. One morning, he was in his usual position, waiting. He'd been there almost an hour and he was rigid with boredom. James came down to breakfast. There was a bang, and Perry jumped; James had trapped a mouse under his cereal bowl. He claimed it had been standing behind Perry laughing at him. The score now stood at five to three.

Perry became obsessed.

*

Perry had a call from his ex-girlfriend:

'Hi.'

'Uh . . . ?'

'It's me.'

'Uh . . .'

'Jasmine.'

'Oh. Hi.'

'Hi.'

'Long time no see.'

'Well, yeah.'

'Listen, can you do me a favour?'

'Uh . . .'

'I need a man.'

'Um . . . Jasmine, I thought . . .'

'There's a mouse. It's in the kitchen. We've shut the door and we think it's trapped. We can hear it moving round in there. We need a man to kill it for us. We can't do anything. We can't even make a cup of tea.'

James was in the lounge reading Marcuse as Perry charged through, heading for the kitchen. 'Who was that?'

'Jasmine.'

'I thought she was history.'

Perry came charging back, clutching the big kitchen carving knife. He gave an evil laugh. He ran to his room, reached under the bed and brought out a three-foot sword. It was an old World War One bayonet that his grandfather had brought back from the occupation of Samoa. Perry had restored it himself, and it had taken him hours and hours of diligent work. Grinding and polishing, polishing and grinding, honing and oiling. It was shiny and sharp as a razor.

'Say hi from me,' called James as the front door slammed.

Jasmine's eyes were round when she saw him on the doorstep.

'My, that's a long sharp sword you have there,' she said.

'Tools of the trade,' he explained casually. 'He'll probably be under the stove, and the knife mightn't reach.' He held up the carving knife to illustrate his point.

'Whatever you say,' said Jasmine. 'Looks like I called the right man, anyhow.' She stepped back to let him in. She was looking good, he noted. Very good in fact. Very, very good. He hadn't seen her for about eight months. Then she'd been about three stone heavier than she was now. Now, she was gorgeous.

'You look great.'

'Eggs,' she said.

'How's that?'

'I went on an egg diet. I ate nothing but eggs for four months.'

'You're kidding me.'

'I kid you not, kid.' She gave him a grin. He knew that grin.

'Well, they worked, that's for sure.' He gave her a grin he thought she might recognise, too, as he stepped across the threshold. 'All right, where's this little fucker hiding?'

The kitchen door was cool against his ear. The house behind him was silent. Jasmine's flatmate had gone out before he arrived (by prior arrangement?) and Jasmine had scurried off to hide in her bedroom while the killing was going on. Perry eased the door open, slipped inside, and shut the door quickly behind him, his heart pounding with anticipation. He looked around the room. It was a perfectly ordinary-looking kitchen. A chrome kettle gleamed on the clean stainless steel bench. The toaster, likewise, was spotlessly shiny. There was a teetering stack of egg cartons on the kitchen table. Free range, size six.

Quietly, Perry laid the sword on the bench by the toaster and crept across the room, looking to the right and left, the carving knife clutched in his right hand, ready to pounce. But when Perry saw it he didn't pounce. Instead he jumped backwards and clutched at a chair, suppressing a scream. It wasn't a mouse, it was a rat. It was in a corner, watching him. An enormous furry rat with a long naked tail trailing behind it across the floor. Vermin. A wave of instinctive revulsion swept over him and he had a powerful urge to run. The rat shifted slightly, tensed, ready for the next move. This was no mouse. A mouse was a streak across the floor, a flurry of movement. But this, this was an animal, crouching in the corner, watching him, planning its moves, ready to fight for its life. This was *personal.*

He was going to need the sword. Keeping his eyes on the rat, he backed slowly across to the bench and felt around behind him. His hand closed on the knurled grip, and courage flowed up his arm. He held the shining steel up in front of him. He was going to kill this rat. He was going to kill it dead. He was going to smash the fucker to smithereens and then by God he was going to fuck Jasmine. He was going to do it.

He gripped the sword, and bared his teeth. A battle cry came up from somewhere deep inside him, and filled the room. 'Ahhhhhhh!!' He lunged at the rat, thrusting with the sword. The point bit lino. The rat was no longer there. Answering his cry with a piercing squeak of its own, it jumped practically halfway across the room to the kitchen door. But the kitchen door was closed. The rat spun on its heels and snarled.

This was going to be no easy victory. Horror rose again in his gullet but he fought it down. Slowly, the sword held in front of him, he advanced, white-knuckled. His legs were trembling. The rat crouched, and a sudden horrifying image flashed into his mind; the rat leaping at him, fastening on his neck, its small sharp teeth digging into his throat, claws scrabbling against his chest. What could you catch from a rat? Bubonic plague? Or was it typhus? He leapt forward again, swinging the sword in a wild slashing arc. Again, the rat easily evaded the blade, but his follow-through caught the egg cartons on the table. They scattered across the floor, oozing egg. Perry blinked.

'Fuck.' He stared at the mess.

Pandemonium broke loose. Perry stormed around the room, cutting, slashing, thrusting, stamping, screaming, in a berserker rage. The rat was a beast possessed. It bounced off walls and floor like a rubber ball, squeaking with fear and rage. Even in the midst of the storm, he marvelled at its agility. The blitzkrieg lasted for less than a minute. Chairs were overturned, cupboard doors smashed and chunks of lino flew. The toaster skittered across the floor, walls and floor were daubed with gobbets of egg. But still the rat stayed clear of Perry's blade, and somehow managed to squeeze through a crack behind a set of cupboards at floor level.

Perry stopped, panting with exertion. There was quiet, dead quiet. He wiped his brow. Listening, he thought he could hear movement inside the cupboard.

'Is . . . is everything all right in there?' Jasmine was calling through the closed door.

'Fine,' he shouted back. His voice cracking. 'Be out in a minute.'

He crept to the cupboard door, tensed, and flung it wide. There it was, crouched on a tin of tomatoes. Grimly, silently, Perry thrust with the sword, again and again. He kept missing, but the rat was in trouble and they both knew it. It had made a grave tactical error. Now that it was in there, there was no way it could get out again, without turning its back. For a vital half second it would be vulnerable and defenceless. The rat was trapped in the cupboard like a—well, like a rat.

His arm aching, his body pouring with sweat, Perry thrust again and again. It was a nightmare. Would nothing kill the beast? The back wall of the cupboard was a mass of holes. Still the rat leapt and ducked and dodged. It was tiring, but so was

Perry. He wasn't aiming anymore, he just kept thrusting blindly, wildly, trusting to luck.

His luck came in as the rat's ran out. He impaled it, right through the middle of the belly. The rat screamed. He shouted, dropped the sword and jumped back across the room. He crouched behind the overturned table, sickened, fascinated, horrified. The rat kicked and scrabbled, scrabbled and kicked, then lay, squeaking faintly, stuck on the end of the sword like a four-legged shish kebab, gouts of rat's blood leaking darkly across the tomato soup tins. Please, please God let it die, prayed Perry. A hind leg trembled a couple more times, then it was still.

Perry felt as if he was recovering from a major illness. His legs were weak and rubbery, his body drenched with sweat. He wanted to be sick. Looking at his hand, he realised he was holding the carving knife in a death grip. He couldn't even remember picking it up. The rat lay still. For a long, long time he stared at the dead rat. He looked around the room. It was a bomb-site. Smashed cutlery, chairs and table overturned, gouges out of the floor, and paintwork, egg smeared everywhere.

'Did you get it?' Jasmine's voice came tentatively through the door.

Perry jumped. 'Uh . . . yeah, yeah, I got it.' Hurriedly, he wiped his face, put down the knife and stuck his head round the door.

Jasmine was standing in the hallway, looking worried. 'Sounded like World War Three in there.'

Perry was working hard on his face muscles. 'Yeah, yeah, bit of a big bastard. Turned out he was a rat.'

'Ugh. A rat?'

'Yeah, put up a bit of a fight, but we got him in the end.'

'Did he go under the stove?'

'No, not as it happens, no, he didn't end up going there.'

'Did you have to use the sword?' Jasmine wrinkled her nose.

'Excuse me.' He staggered to the bathroom, turned back in the doorway. 'Don't go in there.'

'Don't worry.'

The bathroom door was firmly shut behind him. He hung his head over the lavatory. Nothing happened. He washed his face and hands, several times. He could feel disease crawling over his body. He wanted a bath badly, he wanted to bathe in alcohol, he wanted to burn his clothes, he wanted to shave his entire body, and scrub until the skin was raw, but he had a job to do first. He went back to the hall.

'Okay. I need a bucket, a mop, paper towels, hot water, soap . . . and rubber gloves.'

'In the laundry. Back in a sec.' She started for the door, then turned back. 'Hey, thanks.' She grinned up at him. 'Some things you just need a guy for.'

'Well, we do have our uses.'

'Want to stay for dinner?'

'I'm not really that hungry, eh.'

'We don't have to eat.' She sauntered away, swinging her hips.

Perry sat down in the hall and tried to pull himself together. His hands were shaking like leaves. Come on, he told himself, snap out of it. You got it. You nailed the fucker. Right through the middle. Pat on the back for Perry.

By the time Jasmine came back with the gear, he was beginning to revive. She looked really, really good. He glanced at her wrists but he couldn't see any scars. She handed him the bucket, steaming and sudsy, and he allowed his fingers to brush hers as he took it. She grinned. He grinned. 'I guess I could eat something,' he said.

'I could boil you an egg.'

'Or we could have a smoke first. I've got some heads.'

Her brow wrinkled. 'Well, I don't really do that kind of stuff any more.'

'Oh, sure, sure, sorry. Me neither. Much. I mean. You really do look so much better.'

'Thinner, you mean?'

'Well, yeah, but . . . you know, better.'

'I was a mess last time I saw you.'

He didn't really want to get into all that. That was all in the past. This was the present: Jasmine was standing in front of him, and she was thin again.

'I really missed you, Perry.'

'I missed you too.' Christ, he thought, he did miss her. He reached out to touch her face. She caught his finger with her teeth and gently bit it. Her eyes bored into his.

'Rat,' she said.

'Oh, right,' he said. 'I was forgetting.'

Armed with bucket, mop, gloves, towels etcetera, he tramped towards the kitchen, his spirits rising with each heavy, confident step. At the kitchen door he turned back to Jasmine.

'One more thing—I need a plastic bag.' He was going to take this sucker home. He was going to show it to James, and claim his points. And if a mouse is worth one, by God, this has got to be worth two, at least. He'd argue for three. At the very least, he'd argue for three.

The sword was still sticking out of the cupboard. He stepped forward, gingerly. There it was, impaled, right where he'd left it. He knelt down, and reached out with a gloved hand to ease the limp body off the point of the sword. But his hand stopped in mid-air. The room whirled and there was a buzzing in his ears. *The rat was still breathing*. He stared in horror. It was unmistakable; a gentle, rhythmic rise and fall of the pale cream underbelly. He knelt down and stared. Now that he looked more closely, he could see that the sword had in fact entered the rat obliquely, passing through its body, but at a shallow angle. The rat was injured all right, but it was quite possible that the internal organs were not even damaged. It was even conceivable that were he to remove the sword the rat might be able to make a run for it.

'Oh Jesus.'

The rat lay quietly, ignoring him. Its tiny bead-bright eyes were open. Did rats ever shut their eyes? He began to take the animal in. The long whiskers, the comical protruding incisors, the tracery of blood vessels on the tiny, pink, furled ears. It was still breathing. The pale cream of its underbelly contrasted with the dark grey-brown pelt. The rat licked its lips and moved its head, and with that movement it came to him that the rat was suffering. It was lying, in pain, waiting to die. The rat arched its back. It scrabbled at the tomato tins with its forepaws. It twisted its head.

Perry wailed. He felt a wave of pity and sorrow. He knew what he had to do. It was going to be one of the hardest things he'd ever done. He looked around him. There it was on the bench. He picked it up, and the notches were rough on his palm. Seven notches for seven lives. He knelt down, close to the rat. He held the knife, poised, trembling, over the rat's neck. The rat lay still again. Perhaps it was waiting for blessed release. Feverishly, Perry calculated. It had to be a swift, clean chop. He judged the angle, practised the swing. There wasn't enough room in the cupboard for a good back swing, and it was going to be hard to bring enough force to bear. It had to be instantaneous, the rat must suffer as little as possible. He raised the knife. Goodbye, little brother.

The rat gave a sudden, convulsive heave. It flipped itself right off the end of the sword. Perry screamed as droplets of rat blood spattered his face. The rat dived across the room and out the kitchen door.

Perry charged through the door and ran into Jasmine, who stood rigid in the hallway. They clutched at each other.

'Where did it go?'

Jasmine pointed. A trail of blood ran down the hall and into the bathroom.

Perry crept into the bathroom. The trail led across the black and white linoleum and under the bath.

'A torch, get me a torch.'

He knelt down and shone the torch under the bath. There was no sign of the rat, but the blood trail led to some rotten boards right in the corner. There was a hole. The rat was gone. It had escaped.

Perry sat back on his heels. The torch clattered across the floor.

'What?' said Jasmine, 'Where is it?'

'It's gone,' he said. 'Gone.'

'Oh well,' said Jasmine. 'He won't be back in a hurry, that's for sure.'

There was a line of teddy bears along the window sill. They looked down at him with their bright bead-black eyes, as Jasmine pushed him gently down onto the frilly coverlet.

'Perhaps you'll be more comfortable without these . . .' She worked methodically at his belt, and the leather slapped as it slipped through the buckle. She bent lower, a lock of hair slipping out of place. She glanced up at Perry, quickly, then back down to her work.

Perry lay on his back. He felt numb. There were cracks in the ceiling. Something was stuck in his chest, something hard. He swallowed to try to clear it. Last time he'd seen Jasmine had been after she came out of hospital. He hadn't visited her in hospital but he'd heard, and when she came out, he'd gone round to see her. She was even fatter than she'd been when he dumped her. They drove around for a while, then they'd gone to his place. He wasn't sure whose idea that had been. It had been strange. He'd felt lost and small on top of her. Right in the middle of it, she'd called his name. He hadn't liked that.

He hadn't called her again.

The something was still stuck in his throat. He opened his mouth to cough, and the something escaped. It was a sob. It flew out with a harsh, croaking cry. Soon it was joined by others, a flock of them, wheeling about the room.

Jasmine sat back on her heels. Her forehead wrinkled. She pushed the lock of hair back from her face and looked at him, wondering. 'Are you okay? Perry?'

'I'm sorry,' said Perry. He said it over and over again.

The Jean-Paul Sartre Experience

Nearly all our best men are dead!
. . . I’m not feeling so well myself.

PUNCH

I was at breakfast in the lobby of L'Hotel Occidental, when I picked up a copy of *Paris Match*. 'SHARON STONE: LES HOMMES QUE J'AIME,' said the headline. I nearly choked on my croissant.

I read on. Apparently, Sharon adores Jean-Paul Sartre. He sets her brain on fire. That's what it said. 'Ses mots me brulent.' It was all there, in *Paris Match*. I don't know what it is about the French and Sharon Stone. I don't know what it is about the French and Jean-Paul Sartre. Well, I do: the French admire any man whose books are thicker than they are wide, and they adore any woman who doesn't wear underpants.

I read on. Other favourites are Gérard Dépardieu—well, they had to get a Frenchman in there somewhere—Magic Johnson, the Dalai Lama and Jack Nicholson. Michael Douglas is missing from the list, and I put this down to excessive tongue action in *Basic Instinct.* If you haven't seen it, don't. It's disgusting. Poor Sharon.

So, Michael was off the list. Gérard, however, is 'unbelievably sexy and talented.' But Sharon's 'greatest joy'—and I find this rather peculiar—is 'looking into the Dalai Lama's face'. There's a photograph of him on the facing page, the Dalai Lama. Maybe he doesn't photograph well.

In any case, this time *Paris Match* have got it wrong. It's Jean-Paul Sartre Sharon really adores. I see them everywhere. They hang out in cafés, they hang out in bars, they're always together. It's an embarrassment.

Jack Nicholson? 'I love his smile and insight.'

'Magic est mon héros.'

But what I really wanted to know was, where did that leave me?

An embarrassing incident: I was lunching with a friend. A business lunch. I said to him: 'I don't like Jean-Paul Sartre.'

'Is that so?' he said to me.

'That's right. What does he do? He writes thick books. Thick books with catchy titles that nobody reads. *Being and Nothingness.* I mean for goodness' sake.'

'What's wrong with it?'

'What does it mean, *Being and Nothingness*?'

'You'd have to read it.'

'Exactly. And that's what he relies on; no one's going to be stupid enough to pick up a book that thick. They'd strain something before they'd even opened it. Half the pages are probably blank.'

'Are you ready to order?'

'And another thing. The man has no sense of propriety. I saw him and Sharon Stone down the Café Something-or-Other just this morning. In public. Worse than Michael Douglas.'

'You do know he's dead?'

'Michael Douglas?'

'Jean-Paul Sartre.'

I couldn't believe it. 'When did this happen?'

'1971.'

I felt awful. I had no idea. 'Well in that case, who was that I saw with Sharon?'

'That, my friend, I cannot tell you.'

We talked business. But all the time I was thinking about Sharon, and who that man with her could have been. He certainly looked like Jean-Paul Sartre. After lunch I went straight back to the hotel and phoned Sharon.

'Who was that man I saw you with at the Something-or-Other?'

'Depends,' said Sharon, cool as a cucumber. 'Might have been the Dalai, I've been hanging with him a lot these last few weeks.'

'No, it wasn't the Dalai. I'd recognise him.'

'Gérard Dépardieu?'

'No . . . and it wasn't Jack Nicholson or Magic Johnson either.'

'Well, gee,' said Sharon, 'I don't know what to say. Can you describe him?'

'Short. Very dark, Latin-looking. A lot of rings. A bluish tinge around the mouth.'

'Oh,' says Sharon, 'that was Jean-Paul Sartre.'

'But he's dead.'

'I know, isn't it sad?'

Sad? Sharon Stone hanging around with a dead man. I suppose you could say that was sad.

'What about Simone?'

There was a silence. I'd irritated her. 'What about Simone?'

'Aren't she and Jean-Paul supposed to be together or something?'

'Of course they're together.'

'So . . . ?'

Sharon sighed elaborately. 'Since you ask, Albert, I've met Simone, I've talked to her about it, she's very nice, and she doesn't have a problem. Okay?'

'Doesn't have a problem with what, Sharon?'

'Look, don't get your knickers in a twist, it's nothing. It's purely contingent.'

'*Contingent*?'

'Jean-Paul and I have talked about it, Simone and I have talked about it, everyone's talked about it, everyone's cool.'

'Contingent?'

'Look, just don't worry about it, okay?'

'But I do worry, I worry about you.'

'Don't. I can look after myself.'

She practically hung up on me.

I lay on my bed in my room in L'Hotel Occidental. I stared at the ceiling fan. I don't know. Maybe I was overreacting. Traffic outside my window. The panes trembled. The smell of rotting cabbage wafting up from the street. Striped light through the venetians. I just didn't know any more. My friends going around with dead people. Never calling me. They don't remember my birthday. They barely recognise me on the street.

Movement in the corridor outside: muffled laughter, a man and a woman. A truck passes and the whole room trembles. There's a glass of wine on my bedside table half drunk and half full and that's me to a T. I've got to get out, mix, make some new friends. But I don't want new friends, I want the old ones. I want Sharon. Trembling panes. Rotting cabbage. Bubble and squeak.

*

I pulled myself together, had a shower and got in to the Something-or-Other at eight. It was the last place I'd seen Sharon; the last place in the world I should have been. I saw some people I knew, but I avoided them. I was drinking alone.

'Albert!' My heart jumped. It was Sharon, of course. She looked stunning as she flowed across the room in a water-coloured dress. There was a corpse on her arm. 'Albert, this is Monsieur Jean-Paul Sartre. Jean-Paul, this is Albert, a very, very old friend of mine.' She put a hand on my sleeve. Sartre said nothing, but he gave me a crooked, glassy-eyed grin and a mock salute. He looked ghastly. His face was bright blue and he was drinking vodka straight from the bottle. His clothes were tattered and greasy, his hair was all over the place. What could I do? I smiled, I shook hands, I pointed to a seat. Some other people who I didn't know came over—you never get Sharon to yourself—and before I knew it there was a party happening. Great hilarity.

It was pretty dire, really. Sartre told us a long boring story about a brothel he and Simone had visited once in Casablanca. Sharon laughed like a drain at everything he said. As far as I was concerned she was making an absolute fool of herself. It was depressing. Sartre was drinking at an incredible rate—a bottle of vodka to my glass of champagne. And then, when Sharon was in the lavatory, he tried to borrow money off me—he leaned over and gave me what he thought was a conspiratorial grin. Even his gums were blue, and his eyes were dull and dry, like fish you shouldn't buy.

''Ave you by any chance a few thousand francs, mon vieux? Just to get me through to Thursday.'

'What happens on Thursday? They paying out on your life insurance?'

He knew I was trying to insult him, but he just grinned that horrible glassy grin. Cards on the table time. 'Listen,' I said, 'Jean-Paul, I've got nothing against you personally, but

Sharon is a very good friend of mine.'

'Alors?'

'I don't want to see her get hurt.'

'She is a big girl.'

'Listen, Sartre. You do anything to hurt her, anything at all, and I'll kill . . .' I trailed off.

'You were saying?'

'. . . just watch it, okay?'

Sharon came back. She went over behind Sartre and draped herself, chin resting on top of his head. 'Guess where M. Sartre and I are going?' she said.

'I give in,' I said. 'Where?'

'Moscow.'

'Moscow? What in God's name for?'

'Just a holiday.'

'Ah, oui, La Russe . . .' Sartre smiled. 'I have not been there since ze early 1960s. Simone and I dined with Comrade Krushchev in his dacha by the Volga.' I watched Sharon closely at mention of Simone, but she didn't flinch. Sartre continued. 'Krushchev was rather dull, but ze grouse was superbe.'

Sharon took my arm. 'Why don't you come with us?'

'Oh, you don't want me along.'

'Sure we do. Don't we Jean-Paul?'

Sartre grinned maliciously and shrugged.

'How about it, Albert? C'mon, you need a break, you're stressed to hell. We'll take my jet, it'll be fun.'

To abandon Sharon Stone to her fate in the disintegrating capital of the third world with a dead third-rate French socialist free-loving fellow-traveller with no scruples, no money and no prospects? Or to accompany Sharon Stone to the disintegrating as above?

Sharon was waiting.

I raised my glass. Sartre raised his bottle. 'To Moscow.' Sharon wrinkled her nose at me. She leaned over and kissed

Sartre right on the mouth. Very Michael Douglas. Very depressing. The evening was at an end.

The flight was hell. She was all over him, and as for Sartre, I could tell he was playing with her. He didn't really care. All he cared about was vodka. For some reason he seemed to be much more interested in winning my regard.

'Regarde! Albert!' he'd say, 'I see birch trees down there. Not far to go.'

We weren't even halfway across Poland. I said nothing.

''Ave you, by any chance, read any of my books?'

'I read *La Nausée*.' I'd read half of it.

'Ah ha!' He rubbed his hands. 'And what did you think?'

'I was pretty young at the time.'

He looked downcast. 'So was I, mon ami, so was I.' Sartre went back to the window and no one said anything for a while. Maybe I was being a bit harsh. I cleared my throat.

'It was . . . interesting.'

He perked up.

'But there was one thing.'

'Yes?' He sat forward, frowning intelligently.

'Oh, it doesn't matter.'

'No, no, please, mon ami, I would very much appreciate your fine criticisms.'

'Well . . . I don't know if I should say . . .'

'Go on, go on,' he laughed gaily, 'I can take it like a man.'

'Well the main guy, what's his name?'

'Roquentin, Antoine Roquentin. Yes?' He nodded vigorously, serious and receptive.

'Why doesn't he just, I don't know—get a life?'

Possibly not the most tactful way of putting it. Sartre went a paler shade of blue and ran a hand through his thinning hair. When he brought his hand down, a large clump had come away, caught in the setting of the amethyst on his left pinkie. He flicked it away irritably. 'But surely you see . . .'

'Don't worry. I probably just didn't get it.'

'No, no, mon ami, that is a very interesting comment. It is just that . . . you see, I am attempting in the roman, the novel, to explicate the existential dilemma of life . . .'

'But he just seems to moan all the time, about—nothing at all.'

'It is not Nothing that he moans about, it is Being.'

'Whatever.'

Jean-Paul went back to the window.

'Hey,' said Sharon. She was leaning on a stack of cushions, in a tracksuit, fluffy slippers and reading glasses, with a copy of *Being and Nothingness* propped on her knee. 'You can read it after me.' I wasn't telling Sartre, but I did glance at it once. No story. None. 'Anyone want a game of chess?' Sharon looked at Sartre. Sartre looked at me.

'Not me.' No way was I going to play chess with these people.

Sartre looked disappointed. 'What other games 'ave you got, ma chérie?'

'Twister, Snakes and Ladders, or Paintball.' She slinked over and lay across Sartre's lap. She seemed to be incapable of having a conversation without draping herself all over him. Anyway, the thought of watching Sharon and Dead-Boy play Twister was too disgusting to countenance. As for Snakes and Ladders—there's something so depressing about games of pure chance. And Paintball? At thirty thousand feet?

'Albert?' She'd found the hair clump and she was trying to stick it back on.

'I think I'll go and talk to the pilot.'

'Alors, ma chérie, Paintball it is.'

You should have seen the state of the cabin by the time we touched down.

*

Sheremetevo was a nightmare. The queue went forever and when we finally got to the front the guard kept Sharon waiting even longer than usual, just so he could stare at her. He stared and stared, until Sharon said something. Whatever she said, he blushed and let her through. I realised she could speak Russian. Was there anything this woman couldn't do? For a while it looked as if Jean-Paul wasn't going to be so lucky, but once he produced his death certificate the guard was happy to stamp him through as a parcel. I got through, but it cost me. The guard looked at my passport.

'Albert,' he said, using my first name with an irritatingly familiar smirk.

'Yes?'

'You have many peyans?'

'I beg your pardon?'

'Albert, Albert. You are rich man, Albert? Yes? You have many peyans?'

He held something up, and I understood. He was trying to write with the innards of a Bic, the little whippy bit on the inside that holds the ink. It was almost empty. I handed him mine, which was a rather nice Stabilo, and he filled out my visa. Of course I never saw it again.

The baggage hall *looked* like any ordinary airport baggage hall—pictures of diamonds and Rolexes, baggage carousels, cigarette kiosks, and so on. But this was no airport baggage hall. The carousels were empty. The kiosks were closed. Travellers bundled in overcoats and carrying string bags circulated aimlessly, waiting. The wait went on and on. We cycled from boredom to impatience to hilarity to hysteria to apathy and back to boredom again. Sharon was playing 'scissors, paper, string' with Sartre. She was giggling a lot and grabbing his hand and falling all over him every time someone won, which is to say, for those who've never played the game, every three seconds.

I sent my mind elsewhere. I found myself staring at a huge illuminated Marlboro advertisement on the side of a kiosk. I couldn't put my finger on it but there was something about the Marlboro Man's face that was not quite right. I began to wonder if this really was the Marlboro Man at all. It looked the same: moustache, big white hat, dried up lizard-like skin, lasso. But his eyes, there was something about them, a sinister quality, a weakness, a perverted sensuality in their too-blue stare. It was the way he might look if someone had just told you that the Marlboro Man is in fact an aficionado of kiddie porn.

Several aeons later, there was a flurry at the end of the hall. People were crying out, pushing forward in a mass. Airport staff wheeled a caravan of huge baggage trolleys through the crowd and unloaded them, manually, onto the motionless carousels. We dived in with the rest, retrieved our bags and joined the customs queue. Only this wasn't a queue as we know it. We were packed, shoulder to shoulder, in a huge pyramid-shaped mass, shuffling slowly forward towards the tiny bottleneck of the customs gate. The pressure of neighbouring shoulders increased exponentially as we got closer; the weakest were forced out to the sides. In the middle of the crush, when it was quite impossible to move, someone shouted out: 'Sherryn!'

I looked around, but everyone was looking at us. A young man with a hook nose, who was pressed against Sharon's left shoulder, went bright red and started to blather in Russian. He was getting more and more excited. Pens and paper appeared in a dense forest. Sharon started smiling and scribbling. There was another shout and a guy in a stone-wash business suit began to scramble across the heads of the crowd. 'Sherryn! Sherryn!' he screamed. The hook-nosed young man looked over his shoulder, saw Stone-Wash, and turned back to Sharon with renewed urgency. He blathered louder and faster.

He began to bleat and his fingers were plucking at her coat. Sharon looked around, worried. I had to do something. I lunged forward, and succeeded in interposing myself between Sharon and the hook-nosed man, who burst into tears and shouted at me. Stone-Wash was getting closer.

'Take the left,' I ordered Jean-Paul. We packed down and hurled ourselves forward. Sartre was worse than useless. No strength in his muscles. He ended up trailing along behind as we forced a way through to customs. Strangely, no one objected. Maybe they were used to it. Maybe they'd noticed Sartre and were worried about hygiene. Stone-Wash didn't do so well; I looked back just in time to see a large hairy hand reach up and pull him down into the crowd. There was a muffled scream.

The only complication at customs was that passport control had got it wrong. Sartre wasn't a parcel, and one of us had to declare him as a bio-medical product. Sharon already had duty to pay on her cosmetics case, so it fell to me. This meant taking responsibility for his luggage as well, and of course they had to open it up. Forty-seven bottles of vodka, and a lobster. The lobster was live. They hit me for the vodka, and they wanted to class the lobster as an agricultural import too, but I told them it was lunch.

We were in Russia. The arrivals hall was huge, dirty and dim. Tattooed men in fur hats and stretch jeans skulked around the walls, cigarettes peeking out from under their walrus moustaches. Another twenty-foot Marlboro Man leered from a central atrium wall. Through a row of dirty windows, a shrunken sun hung above the horizon. I looked at my watch. It was three-thirty, local time.

There was a shout behind us. I looked around. It was Stone-Wash. He had a bleeding nose, and he was hobbling towards us, shouting in Russian. He looked angry. I prepared to defend myself, but suddenly, out of nowhere, appeared a red streak. It was a man in a red jacket—he went for Stone-Wash like a terrier after a rat, and the dog resemblance intensified when he bit him on the nose. Stone-Wash fled, yelping. The Red Streak loped towards us, wiping his mouth. He was small, with a long thin nose and blocky teeth. Huge fish-like eyes behind greasy wire-rimmed spectacles. David Bowie on a bad hair day. The jacket glittered as he moved, and it had 'Ferrari Racing' embroidered on the back. Before anyone could move he knelt at Sharon's feet and laid a hand on his heart. He looked up at her and said something in Russian. Sharon giggled.

I fumbled for my phrase book. I was looking for something along the lines of 'you cannot win our hearts by violence', but I never got the chance.

'Miss Stone?'

A man was standing near the main doors. He appeared to have witnessed the whole thing, and he was grinning broadly. Just behind him stood two more men in dark glasses and long coats. He himself was in high leather boots, tight grey trousers and a karakul greatcoat. A giant, almost as broad as he was high, he reminded me of one of Jean-Paul's books. Slavic cheekbones, dark, slanted eyes, fingers like salamis. He lifted a finger, and Red Streak slunk to one side.

'Allow to introduce myself,' he said, in thickly accented English. 'I am Alexei III, rightful head of royal house of Romanov and heir to throne of Russia, in accordance with sacred doctrine of divine right of kings, tracing my inheritance in unbroken line of succession stretching back to days of Rurik and beyond.'

He paused for breath. 'However, none of this is relevant. I greet you today in my capacity as chairman of All-Russia Society of International Friendship and Humanitarian Co-operation. We welcome you, Sherryn Stone, to our glorious capital. Welcome to the city of a thousand churches.' He put a hand on his heart and bowed.

Sharon, looking very much at home, extended her hand. He took it and kissed it. 'Madame Stone, I have for long admired your cinematic performance in *Basic Instinct.*' He smiled and moved closer. 'Tell me, please, is it true that in this film you are not wearing underpants?'

Sharon's reply was charming and relaxed. 'You'll have to forgive me, Your Highness, I never discuss underwear on a first acquaintance.'

'Of course. Forgive me.' Clearly we were dealing with a gentleman. Next he turned inquiringly to Jean-Paul. Sharon did the introductions.

'Allow me to present M. Jean-Paul Sartre.'

'Indeed? You are, sir, French socialist philosopher, author of so many highly influential and bulky publications?'

Jean-Paul nodded.

'And, also, a personal friend of Nikita Krushchev?'

Jean-Paul nodded.

'A committed Marxist and fellow-traveller?'

Jean-Paul nodded vigorously.

Alexei narrowed his eyes. His voice rumbled menacingly. 'I say once and once only. Marx was idiot. Lenin was murderer. You, who have never lived with consequences of actions of these two buffoons, cannot possibly understand.' He looked closely at Jean-Paul. 'But you are, I think, artist. You understand suffering, understand the saul.' He banged his chest with a huge fist. 'I think, yes, we can be friends.' He clasped Jean-Paul in a bear-hug, then sprang back in horror.

'The Devil! This man is cold! Cold as ice!'

'M. Sartre has unfortunately been deceased for some years now.'

Alexei shrugged. 'Is not important.' He jerked a thumb at the young man in the red jacket. 'Sergei, my nephew. He is genius computer geek. He would die for you.' He addressed this to Sharon.

'Some of us already have.' I couldn't resist. Sartre squared his shoulders. The young man said something in Russian.

'Well, well, he says he's my number one fan in Russia,' said Sharon.

'Number one fen,' repeated Sergei, unsmiling.

'Sergei is world first,' said Alexei. 'He is maintainer of world's only all-Russian language Sherryn Stone weyeb site.'

'Weyeb site,' Sergei repeated. He looked at Sharon, his eyes blazing. 'Sherron sent from Gourd.'

Sharon nodded politely and, as an afterthought, gestured to me. 'Oh, and this is Albert, my driver.'

I was so stunned I couldn't speak. Alexei flashed me a micro-smile and made his majestic way to the doors. The two men in dark glasses closed ranks behind and Sergei followed, walking backwards so he could keep his eyes on his goddess.

I found my tongue. 'What did you just call me?'

Sharon made her eyes round. 'You don't mind do you, Al?'

'Mind?' I was furious.

'Don't worry,' she said, 'no one's actually going to make you drive or anything.'

'Then why did you call me your driver?'

'Don't be silly. This is an official visit. I had to tell them you were something.'

'Official? I thought this was a holiday!'

'Well, semi-official.'

'What do mean, semi-official?'

'A kind of official holiday.'

'What the hell's going on? Who is this man? What haven't you told me?'

Sharon looked vague. 'Nothing, nothing. I just have to present an award.'

'What award?'

'Just some award. I don't know.'

'I still don't see why I can't just be me. He can.' I pointed to Sartre, who developed a sudden interest in the view outside the window.

Sharon looked at me with pity. 'For God's sake, Albert, he's Jean-Paul Sartre.'

'That does it. I'm leaving.'

'Oh c'mon, don't you get on your high horse. It'll be fun. Anyway, I need you.' She adjusted my collar. I crumbled.

Outside was a muddy car park and a concrete overpass. The sky was mud-coloured. In the distance was a concrete tower. Everything was the colour of concrete, or mud. Or muddy concrete. The air smelt of low-grade petrol.

'Please.' Alexei, flanked by the men in dark glasses, gestured in the direction of a car. It was a long low black limousine. It had Flash Gordon fins, white wall tyres and a grill like a tyrannosaurus in orthodontics. It had a little flag on the bonnet, stiffened with wire—the two-headed eagle of the Russian empire. There was a cheerful-looking sticker on the bumper, with one of those red 'heart' symbols. I asked Jean-Paul for a translation: 'Honk if You Love the Tsar!'

Alexei patted the vehicle. 'A Chaika. Genuine ex-government model. This one was personal car of Gorbachev when he was young man, in Stavropolski Krai.'

'It's gorgeous.' Sharon slipped with practised seductiveness into the back compartment, followed by Jean-Paul, who was giggling uncontrollably. The two guys in sunglasses jumped into a jeep, parked behind the Chaika. There were two more in the back seat.

I went to follow Sharon, but Alexei tut-tutted: 'Wrong seat, Albert.' He threw something at me. I caught it: it was a chauffeur's cap.

We were following a slushy, pot-holed highway. There were dead fields on either side, strewn with muddy, unmelted snow drifts. In the distance was Moscow. The rays of the setting sun, directly over the city, reached through the haze like a drowning man. In front of me, my white-knuckled hands clutched a steering wheel which must have been salvaged from the Titanic. The car handled like the Titanic too. If you put on the brakes it stopped about twenty minutes later. Beside me sat Sergei, hunched, glaring straight ahead. He was sulking because he'd thought he was to be Sharon's chauffeur. Personally I would have been quite happy.

Jean-Paul, Alexei and Sharon were chatting in the back, weaving from language to language. I caught fragments.

'. . . the Mafia run everything nowadays . . . they run the banks, they run the government, they run the aid organisations . . . people starve on the streets . . . old people starve in their homes . . . if they have homes . . . no one knows what they're doing any more . . . except the Mafia . . . they know what everyone's doing . . . but no one's doing anything . . . it's a farce . . . it's a tragedy . . . it's a farcical tragedy, a tragi-comedy . . . a farcical tragi-comic satirico-historical revenge play with aspects of situation comedy . . .'

We entered the outskirts of the city and began to fight our way through heavy traffic, down endless, dismal, dual carriage-ways. This was the season of slush. Everywhere was slush. Ankle-deep, thigh-deep, hip-deep. The city was one gigantic filthy snow-cone.

Driving in Russian traffic turned out not to be so bad. Other cars made way for the limousine, as if by instinct. Perhaps it was something to do with the escorting jeep. But the car stuck out so far in so many unexpected directions that I was just as likely to sideswipe a building or a pedestrian as another car. The road rules weren't just unfamiliar, they were perverse. Every intersection had its own set of rules, completely different from every other intersection. Alexei expended more energy shouting last-minute instructions at me than he would have if he'd driven himself: 'Here, Albert, here, after the bridge, we wish to turn left. Therefore, you must turn right—NO, NO,

RIGHT, QUICKLY, QUICKLY CHANGE LANES NOW—good, now go back under bridge, turn right again, go through carriageway in front of you, and then and only then, may you turn left . . .'

We began to approach the city's heart. Once-magnificent buildings, with arched carriageways and crumbling nineteenth-century façades lurked shoulder to shoulder, lining the grand boulevards. The footpaths were crowded now, with fast-moving figures, bundled in overcoats, hats and scarves. Everyone was carrying something. A parcel, a package, a case. Kiosks lined the streets, advertising Swedish Vodka. The Marlboro Man looked down from vast billboards, his eyes sardonic, unsmiling, triumphant.

Sometimes people stopped to watch as we went by, and some pointed and waved. Once or twice someone even tooted, and then Alexei would frantically stick his head out the window, waving and shouting. He explained he had a friend with an arc welder who was going to cut a hole in the roof so he could wave with proper dignity.

My attention wavered, as the conversation continued:

'The Russian saul . . . the suffering of the people . . . the revolution . . . revolution in the revolution . . . return of the monarchy . . . fourteen to the dollar . . . the Russian church . . . a great man, truly . . . the saul of the Russian people . . . Arthur Hailey . . . a spiritual people . . . marijuana . . . Napoleon . . . last of the Romanovs . . . American dollars . . . Pushkin . . . sight-seeing . . . fifteen to the dollar . . . my mother has an apartment . . . girls, boys, whatever you want, it's all the same . . . photocopier . . . cocaine . . . all right sixteen . . . ex-nuclear scientist . . . all right all right seventeen . . . sells apples in the street . . . my sister . . . my brother . . . my father . . . my cousin . . . eighteen and that's as far as I go . . .'

With a cold feeling in my stomach, I began to realise just how far I had already come. This was unknown territory. I didn't know the language, I didn't know the way back, I didn't know which way to turn at the next intersection. How far would I get, I wondered, if I was left to my own devices, to bargain my way at fifteen apples to the nuclear scientist? How far would I get?

It was dark by the time the Chaika limped down to the river, and swung into the forecourt of the Rossiya Hotel. I was exhausted, drenched in sweat. My hands trembled on the wheel. I pulled on the handbrake, and got out. The roar of traffic came from across the river. The night air was cold and a moist wind blew. Intermittent needles of sleet stung my cheek. I squinted up into the gathering darkness. The hotel towered over us. Far, far above, a huge red neon star blinked and stuttered.

'Welcome to the Hotel Rossiya,' said Alexei.

'My God,' I said under my breath, 'what a joint.'

Jean-Paul was beside me. 'Alexei says it is ze biggest hotel in Europe.'

'The biggest *joint* in Europe.'

Alexei and Jean-Paul went inside. Sharon went to follow but I drew her aside. Sergei stood at a short distance, staring. I whispered, urgently.

'We have to dump this guy.'

'Alexei? C'mon, lighten up. He's fun.'

'He thinks he's the tsar.'

'He probably is. Trust me, this guy's got connections. His cousin's wife's ex-husband is an oligarch.'

'Is that supposed to make me feel better?'

'You don't like any of my friends, do you?'

'I want to go home.'

Sharon patted me on the arm. 'Relax. That's what you're here to do, Albert. Relax.'

'I can't relax in a place like this.'

She put a hand on my arm. 'Give it a day. If you're still not happy tomorrow, I'll fly you home, personally. But you'll enjoy it, you'll see. Godammit, Albert, this is one of the great European capitals.'

'I'm not so sure about Europe these days.'

'Albert, you know what they say. He who is tired of Europe, is tired of life.'

'It was Johnson and he said it about London.'

'London's part of Europe.'

'Not in Johnson's day.'

'Well, anyway, if it applies to a crap hole like London, it goes double for Moscow.' She pecked me on the cheek. 'C'mon, Albert! Balalaikas! Vodka! Onion domes! Fur hats! We're gonna have fun!' She punched my arm and wandered inside. I came through the doors just in time to see her goosing Jean-Paul at the check-in desk. I wanted to cry.

Sharon and Jean-Paul took the penthouse, I was a floor down on the other side of the building. They had a stunning view of Red Square and Saint Basil's, looking across to the Kremlin. I had a view of a tractor park. I unpacked, and lay across the chocolate-coloured bedspread. I was wondering if I'd brought enough clothes; I didn't really have anything warm. What was I thinking of? I stared at the ceiling. Another hotel room in another hotel on the wrong side of Europe. A smell like rotten cabbage coming from the heating ducts, tractor traffic making the double glazing tremble. A sound of muffled laughter in the hall. An antique phone beside the bed began to ring. It was Sharon.

'Your place or mine?' Very funny.

When I left the room, one of Alexei's men was waiting in the corridor, right outside my door. He fell in behind as I made my way to the lift. We stood side by side as the automatic doors closed. He was quite short but he had a weight lifter's neck. He was well dressed, with a wide-brimmed felt hat and a dark suit. His overcoat was well tailored, but it seemed to have an unsightly bulge under the left armpit. All the way up to the thirteenth floor we rode in silence. I kept glancing at the bulge. I couldn't help it.

The bell pinged and the doors slid back. As I stepped out into the lobby, he tapped me on the shoulder. I jumped. He grinned a wide, shark-like grin. He beckoned to me to follow. I followed. Looking right and left, he led me down the corridor and into the gents. The door swung to. My guts felt like water. He checked all the cubicles carefully, then he turned back to me. I noticed a line of pimples on his neck just above the collar. The room was tiled; easier to clean afterwards? He held out the left lapel of his coat. It was there all right, a huge, hideous hand gun in a complicated leather holster.

'*Colt*,' he said. My gaze flickered to his eyes, but there was nothing to see behind the glasses. He smiled and nodded. '*Colt forty-fife*.' I smiled too. He laughed. I laughed. He shrugged. I flapped my hands and slapped my knee, capering like a pantomime horse. Still giggling, I turned to go, but his smile vanished and he stopped me with a gesture. Rigid, I waited for the end. I could hardly stand. He reached for his coat—but the other side of his coat. There was something even bigger on that side. It looked like a small cannon. How could this man walk upright? I realised what I thought had been his aftershave in the lift must have been the smell of gun oil. '*Uzi*.' He said. '*Uzi—aftomat*.'

'Uzi,' I said.

'*Uzi, Uzi*,' he said.

I nodded and smiled and laughed until the tears ran down my cheeks. The left side of my face began to twitch uncontrollably. Again I tried to leave, but again he held up his hand, like a stage magician. I suppressed a sob. He lifted his left trouser leg: '*Beretta*.'

His right trouser leg. '*Bowie*.'

His left sleeve. '*Stiletto.*'

His right sleeve. '*Semtex.*'

His tie. '*Hatpin.*'

His hat. '*Have nice day.*'

I walked down the corridor to the penthouse, trying to hide the weakness in my knees. He followed me, a pace behind all the way. There was another guard outside Sharon's door. Sharon answered.

'Albert, honey, come on in.' She pecked me on the cheek. She was cool and relaxed. She'd changed, and she was holding a cocktail glass—pink champagne. Behind her I could see Alexei sprawled on a leather couch, his boots propped on the armrest.

'Alberchik!' He waved ironically. 'Come in, come in.'

My guard stayed outside, but there were two more just inside the doorway. Sergei was by the drinks cabinet, stiff and unsmiling, his filthy glasses hiding his eyes. If that boy was armed, we were all as good as dead. Sergei with a gun made David Koresh look like Kofi Annan. At least he didn't appear to be drinking.

'Vodka?' Sharon held out a glass and I took it. 'Sergei?' She held out a glass to him, too. Sergei took it, drained it, then slipped it into his breast pocket. Sharon giggled and wandered across to the window, a drunken lilt to her walk. Two pairs of eyes, Alexei's and Sergei's, followed her, one fanatical, one predatory. All right, three pairs.

'Come and look, Albert. It's stunning.'

It was. Floodlit, the Kremlin looked like a fairy-tale castle, and Saint Basil's looked like a pile of brightly painted artichokes. Tiny figures crossed Red Square, moving erratically. 'Where's Jean-Paul?' I asked.

'He's unpacking.'

'You mean he's trying to decide where to put the lobster?'

'Don't be silly. It's not real.'

'Then what's it doing here?'

'Must like him, I guess.'

'Sharon . . .' I leaned closer, whispering, but Alexei was watching.

'What?'

'Nothing.'

She gave me a funny look, and turned back to Alexei, raising her voice. 'You have a beautiful city, Your Highness.'

Alexei spoke carelessly. He clearly had a head start on the vodka. 'Yes. Beautiful. But when I am tsar, capital will be Petersburg again. Only then, will be renamed Alexeigrad. Will be new wonder of world. Pleasure capital of universe.' He saluted Sharon with his glass.

Jean-Paul came out of the bedroom. I was almost glad to see him. His hair was slicked down, and he must have been rummaging in Sharon's makeup kit, because his lips were a ghastly cherry-red now, and his face was painted ski-instructor brown. Unfortunately he'd missed behind his jaw, and the effect was truly horrific, as if he'd been to a cut-price embalmer's. The omnipresent bottle was in his hand.

'Albert!' he came over to us and Sharon's arm slid round his neck. She gave him a kiss. I could see Alexei's eyes bugging out of his head. I had to move away. I sat in an armchair off the end of the couch. Sharon and Jean-Paul gazed out the window, arm in arm, their heads touching. Somehow I had to get Sharon alone, warn her.

Alexei twisted around and beckoned me down to him. He whispered hoarsely, his whiskers tickling my ear. 'Those two, they are—focking?'

I was too revolted to speak. Alexei looked at me shrewdly.

'Albert, little Albert . . . I think you are not just driver.' His mind must have travelled back to the afternoon's journey, because he added, 'In fact, you are not driver at all.' He looked across at Sharon. 'Such a woman should have living man. Yes?

Living flesh.' His massive fists clenched. 'Warm, pulsing with blood, rising to occasion. Yes? Such a woman cannot be satisfied with limp embrace of dead fish, of cold flesh, kisses from grave, taste of decay. Such woman needs touch of living virile man, man who can satisfy needs of woman, such woman . . .'

He paused, breathing heavily. Possibly a touch of angina. I hastened to intervene, trying to sound relaxed and urbane. 'So, what line of business are you in, Alexei?'

He pointed at my chest with a finger as thick as an Uzi barrel. 'Who are you?' he hissed.

'I'm—I'm a friend of Sharon's,' I squeaked.

'Good friend?'

'Pretty good.'

'Do you make together the beast?'

'The, um . . . ?'

'The beast with two backs.' He grinned. His teeth were as big as tombstones.

'Oh, that.'

He leant over and pushed his face into mine. I was enveloped in a miasma of vodka fumes. His eyes were two dull plates of meat. 'She is wearing them? Yes or no? The underpants. Answer me.'

'Please, Prince Alexei . . .'

He growled warningly under his breath.

I began to stammer. 'I have no idea. I am a friend . . . just a friend.'

He stared at me, grunted and looked away. 'Dolls.'

'I beg your pardon?' What horrific form of perversion was he now about to suggest?

'Matrioshka dolls. My line of business. Joint venture. Export Matrioshka dolls. China, America, Scandinavia, Europe, Middle East. All over world.'

'Gosh, how fascinating. Is business good this time of year?'

'Of course is good. We make many thousands of dollars. I

have large account in Birmingham, Alabama. Very large. Many thousand of dollars. Hm, dollars, from dolls.' He laughed at his own joke. 'Alberchik!' He reached up and pounded me on the back. 'Do you know what this means? Alberchik? Little Albert! My little friend! Drink, Alberchik! Viypi! Drink up!'

I drank.

'What's all the noise?' Sharon was looking at us.

'Albert is my little friend, now,' said Alexei. 'He is telling me all about you, Sherryn. All intimate details.'

'And how do you know Albert knows all my most intimate details?'

'He is living man. Is warm to touch. Yes? Do you not crave touch of living man?'

Jean-Paul went to get another drink. He muttered something under his breath. Sharon looked long and hard at Alexei. I was terrified she was going to say something combative. How could I warn her what sort of man she was picking a fight with? One of the goons by the door shifted his weight.

Sharon looked away. 'Don't worry about me, I get my kicks all right.'

Alexei burst out laughing. He sounded like a foghorn.

For the next six hours we sat in a hotel room with Prince Alexei III, last living descendant of the house of Romanov, and drank vodka. Alexei began to work his way through the stages of intoxication. First, the witty phase:

'In a way, you know, nothing has changed in Russia. In old days, were queues outside bread shops. Now: queues outside banks. That is all. But when I am tsar, then all will change.'

Then the not-so-witty phase:

'All those in room who are wearing underpants, put up their hands.'

Then, the sardonic phase:

'Russia. Ha. Russians are so excited by mere fact that is possible to buy, on Moscow street, vodka which isn't Russian, they fail to notice, own Russian vodka is vastly superior product. So they drink Absolut, and they think is good thing. Is like that with books—now they all reading Arthur Hailey. They used to read Tolstoy and Dostoyevsky because was all they could get. Now, Arthur Hailey. McDonald's. Marlboro. Ha! Marlboro. Give me good Russian papirossi.'

Then, passionate:

'The west has only one thing—wealth. They have no culture. They have no saul. No dusha!' (Thumping his chest.) 'Western culture is disease, is plague. I will cure Russia, I will cure my people! Under restored monarchy, Russia will become again, greatest nation on earth!'

I didn't ask when the last time was.

Then, maudlin:

'The Russian people. We have suffered. We have suffered more than the Jews. We are the very spirit of suffering.'

I couldn't let this pass. 'Come now, Alexei.'

'You do not agree with me?'

Jean-Paul tried to join in. 'Speaking as a Marxist . . .'

Alexei pointed without turning his head. 'You. Shut up.'

I tried again. 'What about the six million Jews in the war?'

'Six? Ha! Twenty! Twenty million sauls in the archipelago alone. In the Gulags. I do not even bother to count Great Patriotic War.'

'Some of those were Jews.'

'There are representatives of every nation, creed and colour in Gulag Archipelago. You can check out any time you like. But can never leave. The Eagles. Very spiritual rock group. "Hotel California", this is all about Gulags.'

'"Hotel California" is about Stalinist repression?'

'I read in *N.M.E.*'

'Anyway what's this about every creed and nation?'

'Spiritually speaking. I am a Russian. I am spiritual man.'

Jean-Paul had returned to the window and the view of the

Kremlin. Sharon was asleep on the bed. As I watched, Jean-Paul upended and emptied a full 750 ml bottle of vodka. He looked at the empty bottle and sighed.

'You.' Alexei truculently beckoned Jean-Paul over. 'You, dead French philosopher who drinks like a Russian. Tell me. Is true, that Russian saul is deepest saul in world? That Russians are most spiritual nation on earth?' Jean-Paul shrugged and grinned. 'Listen to me, philosopher. In Russia, word for peace, and word for world, is same word. "Mir." Same word!' Alexei's eyes brimmed with tears. 'Russia! Rossiya! Motherland! Rodina maya!' He was sobbing now, the tears struggling to make headway against the thick stubble on his cheeks. He began to recite something in Russian.

'Pushkin. Naturellement, he recites Pushkin,' said Jean-Paul. 'Would you like me to translate for you, mon ami?'

'Don't bother.'

Maudlin went on for a long time, but it eventually gave way to lecherous:

Alexei looked across at Sharon, who had fallen asleep on the couch. He tried to look up her skirt and fell off his chair. A goon helped him up.

Then came nasty:

'Fuck your mother.' Addressed to no one in particular. His eyes swivelled, glassy and malicious. 'Eh? What did you say? French philosopher?' Jean-Paul hadn't said a thing. 'What? I did not hear you.' Alexei had a menacing note in his voice. He twitched a forefinger. Sergei leapt across the room, and the muzzle of what I instantly recognised to be a Colt forty-fife was pressed against Jean-Paul's forehead. Jean-Paul dryly returned Sergei's manic stare. Sergei looked to Alexei, who shrugged. Sergei pulled the trigger. There was a deafening report. I had no idea that a pistol shot could be so loud. My ears were ringing. Sharon turned over in her sleep. Jean-Paul stared at Sergei with as much dignity as he could muster with a hole in the middle of his forehead. Alexei roared with laughter.

Finally, oblivion:

Alexei pitched slowly off the couch and hit the floor. The goons carried him out, snoring like a train.

I shook Sharon by the shoulder. 'Sharon. For God's sake, wake up.'

She stirred. 'What?'

'Sharon, they're Mafia, all of them. They've just shot Jean-Paul.'

Sharon blinked sleepily. 'Where is he?'

'In the bathroom, patching his forehead.'

'Poor baby.'

'Sharon! They're armed to the teeth. They're dangerous.'

Sharon shrugged and rolled over, snuggling into the cushions. 'What do you expect? They're Mafia.'

'Sharon! We have to get out of here.'

'Don't be silly. They're on our side.'

'What about Jean-Paul?'

'He doesn't mind. Ask him. Alexei was just having fun.'

'He's a paranoid megalomaniac. He thinks the Eagles are spiritual. We must leave, immediately.'

'I can't do that.'

'Why not?'

'I promised.'

'Promised?'

'To present the award, silly.'

'What is this presentation?'

'I think it's a prize.'

'What prize?'

'First prize, of course. I forget. Some damn thing. Doesn't matter.'

'It's probably Best Marksman in a Public Place or Most Consecutive Garrottings.'

'Don't be silly, and don't be so negative all the time. Alexei isn't just a Mafia boss, that's only one aspect of his personality. He's a very capable man.'

'Sure he is. Capable of anything. And what about Sergei? He's a fanatic. Being around you has put him close to meltdown. He's going to crack, it's only a matter of time.'

'I can handle him.'

'Nothing he'd like better.'

'If this conversation's getting vulgar, I'm off to bed. Jean-Paul?' She levered herself to her feet, and went in search of the perforated philosopher. I poured myself a last vodka, and finished the room-service caviar.

I was alone, looking out over the city. The river was slow and black in the distance, glinting here and there like the neck of a broken bottle. Laughter drifted out of the bedroom, light, carefree.

I sat on the couch and buried my face in my hands. It all crowded in on me. Fear, loathing, love, loss, loneliness, jealousy . . .

Something tickled my elbow. It was the lobster. It was sitting in my lap, looking up at me with concern in its stalk-mounted eyes.

'Oh God, what do you want?'

It said nothing, but tut-tutted and scrambled up my shirt, leaping from button to button. It tried to put its little crustacean legs around my neck. There is nothing remotely comforting about the embrace of a lobster, however tenderly it is meant.

I staggered into the hall, and to the lift. There was a skittering noise—the lobster was following me.

'Go away.'

The lobster waved its feelers as we dropped thirteen, fourteen, fifteen, sixteen floors. Down and down. Seventeen . . . twenty . . . forty . . . down . . . down . . . the bell rang and the doors slid back. It was uncomfortably warm.

The largest hotel in Europe has many corridors. Mile upon mile. They are all green. Every mile or so there was an alcove with nothing in it. Full to the gunwales with Russian vodka, I staggered along, careening gently off the green walls. It was like being a billiard ball. I believed then, and I believe today, that all the hotel corridors of all the hotels of all the world, somewhere, via a neglected stairwell or hidden service way, join up. If I walked for long enough, I told myself, I'd be in Paris, L'Hotel Occidental. I'd be in Rome, L'Albergo Occidentale. Or London, The Great Western Hotel. I'd be in Whangarei, at The Dew Drop Inn. I walked and walked down those stuffy green corridors, taking corner after corner, passing empty alcove after alcove, but I couldn't find the connection. It was stifling. The wallpaper began to peel. Behind doors there was whispering and laughter, and the smell of rotten cabbage wafted from somewhere, perhaps from Paris, perhaps from Rome. I was trapped in the Hotel Corridors. You can check in any time you like. But you can never breathe. The alcoves were occupied now: an old woman with a stoven-in head, her white hair matted with blood, counting money; a young man in a ragged coat; an ageing libertine; a girl with a weak neck; a black cat dancing with a naked woman and a man in checked trousers; and at the far end of the corridor a tall man in black hose and patched pyjamas, one eye a black empty hole, the other a cold bright star.

There was a tickling sensation in my palm. The lobster took me by the hand.

'You've taken a wrong turn. Come along. I'll show you to your room.'

'You can talk?'

'It's all right, I'm not real.'

Not such a bad little fellow, after all. I followed my new friend through walls and ceilings, down corridors and up staircases, to a chocolate bedspread. A flurry of snow at the window. A freeze was coming. That can happen, the unexpected freeze. The sudden plummet. I had just the strength to pull myself under the covers. Jesus they've short-sheeted me, the bastards. This is Russia, where you make your own bed. Then lie in it.

I had the nicest awakening I've ever had. Sharon was massaging my hands. It was sublime and gentle. It was a dream. I opened my eyes in time to see the lobster melting through the wall. Pale morning light was filtering through the grubby double glazing. I was lying fully dressed under the chocolate bedspread. I felt full of confidence so I sat up. A pair of giant stag-beetle pincers came out of the wall and impaled both sides of my head.

By the time I made it down to the restaurant, Sharon and Jean-Paul were already breakfasting; Jean-Paul, who had a piece of toilet paper plastered across the hole in his forehead, was onto his second bottle of Stolichnaya. Sharon had her hermetically sealed self-refrigerating salad bag on the table. There was someone with them. A smallish man in a horribly crumpled white linen suit and funny little eye-glasses. He had a goatee. He jumped to his feet as I approached, and stood, bobbing slightly at the waist. He was quite obviously dead as a dodo.

Jean-Paul was beside himself with excitement. 'Albert, puis-je present to you, M. Anton Pavlovich Chekhov!' I did my best to smile and we shook hands. 'Just think,' continued Jean-Paul, 'what a marvellous coincidence, merveilleux! We were just looking for the toilets and I asked for directions, and whom should I address, but Anton Pavlovich himself!' Anton kept smiling his tight little smile, and bobbing forward at the waist. His ears were black.

Jean-Paul stood up and clapped him on the shoulder. 'You are a great artist, monsieur, and I salute you.' Anton smiled and bobbed. Never having had the opportunity to read Jean-

Paul he was at a disadvantage. The latter continued. 'However, I look forward to the opportunity to debate your political position, which I think is insufficiently worked out.'

'Well, you know,' replied Chekhov, 'I was never much interested in politics.'

'But to refuse to take a political position is to play into the hands of reaction.'

'Sleep well?' said Sharon.

The programme for the day had already been decided. The presentation, whatever it was, was scheduled for that night. Sharon still wasn't sure about the exact nature of the award, but it was to be a dinner and dance black-tie occasion at The Idiot, an upmarket restaurant not far from Red Square. Sharon, Jean-Paul and Anton were all set for a day of sight-seeing, and arguing about where we should go first.

'How about The Tretyakov?'

'Non, non, ma chérie, Novodevichy Convent, you will adore it. C'est magnifique.'

Chekhov bobbed and spoke. 'You know, if you would care to visit the Convent, I would be honoured to show to you my personal grave in the world-famous Novodevichy cemetery next door.'

Sharon shrugged. 'Oh, okay. Albert?'

'I'll go along with anything, so long as it doesn't involve Alexei and Sergei.'

We stepped outside. The air was chill, without being fresh, the sky was leaden. The Chaika was parked in the slipway. Sergei was leaning against the bonnet, hands thrust into his pockets, jacket zipped up to the chin, the end of his thin nose red with cold. He hadn't noticed us. Behind the Chaika was the jeep, and on the other side of the slipway was a medium sized crowd. They had banners, and they were calling out: 'Sherryn . . . Sherryn . . .' The four goons were keeping them at bay. Jean-Paul translated some of the banners for me:

WE LOVE YOU SHARON

ALEXEI FOR KING

SHARON MAKE OUR KING A HAPPY MAN

SHARON STONE FOR ROYAL FAMILY

ROYAL FAMILY FOR SHARON STONE

ALEXEI/SHARON = EUGENIC MATCH MADE IN HEAVEN OF OUR DREAMS

SHARON GET ME A XEROX

I thought the last one might have been genuine but the rest were obviously plants.

The electric window on the back of the Chaika slid down, and a familiar face leered in our direction.

'Oh Jesus,' I said, 'just pretend we don't see him. Keep walking.'

'Alexei!' Sharon skipped over, kissed him on the cheek and jumped in the back. Jean-Paul went to follow, but I caught his arm.

'After what they did to you last night? Have you no pride?'

'Mon ami, pride is the last refuge of the living.' He jumped in after Sharon, and Chekhov followed suit. Sergei slung me the keys.

Novodevichy Convent was a collection of white towers and golden onion domes, nestled in a curve of the Moscow River. It was quite beautiful. People were queuing at the gate to buy tickets, but Alexei made me drive right in the main gates, ignoring the apathetic policemen. We lurched to a stop outside the main door of the convent building and followed Alexei as he strode breezily up the steps. No queuing for us. Alexei turned and winked at Sharon. He was obviously out to impress.

'Come, as long as we are here, I will introduce to you our patriarch, Alexei the Second, head of Russian Church. He is old friend.'

The reception desk was manned by a dangerous-looking old woman: a babushka. Because the following exchange struck me as being of considerable ethnographic value, I went to the trouble of getting Jean-Paul to explain it to me in detail. I transcribe it herewith:

[Alexei approaches the desk.]

'Shto viy?' [Who do you think you are?]

'Skazhi mne, babushka, patriarch doma? [Tell me, grandmother, is the patriarch home?]

'K'chyortu! Negadyai!' [Go to the devil. You are a worthless person.]

'Nu shto viy?' [Come now.]

'Von!' [Go away.]

'Pzdyokha!' [You are a woman who farts silently and frequently.]

'Pashol, igraiy billyard f'karmanu.' [Go away and play pocket billiards.]

'Ya vash Tzar!' [I am your king.]

'Idi na khui!'

As Jean-Paul was at pains to explain, this is the most heinous insult it is possible to sustain in the Russian language. Literally translated it means 'go onto the penis'. However the phrase 'get fucked' doesn't begin to reveal its magnificent scope and power. Alexei turned pale. The goons covered their ears. The babushka kicked Alexei in the shins, hustled us all outside and slammed the door. Alexei straightened his clothes. 'Perhaps we will start with cemetery.'

We went out the main gate, followed a high brick wall, and entered the cemetery grounds, which shared a wall with the convent. Bare trees towered above our heads. Underneath them was a dense network of wrought-iron fences, well above waist height, each one enclosing a plot. Inside the small enclosures formed by the fences, were the headstones. A grid system of narrow pathways separated all the enclosures. It was a bit like New York, except everyone was dead and there was no traffic.

'Come, I will show you my grave.' Chekhov led the way, but I hung back. I was in a terrible mood. I was hung-over, Sharon was too busy with the dear departed to pay any attention to me. But worst of all, it was my birthday, and Sharon had obviously forgotten. I'd been waiting all morning for her to say something, but by now it was obvious she wasn't going to.

I let the others go ahead, and before long I was alone among the plots. I wandered, taking corners at random. It was like being a rat in a maze. I looked at the plots on either side. Some were overgrown, some were neatly tended. Some were very old, and some were very new. Many of the headstones were embellished with full colour photographs of the deceased, a large proportion of whom had gaps between their front teeth. I don't know why. The statuary was varied; stone angels vied with jet-fighters. A crow called from the top of a tree, and another answered. They were huge, glossy black birds with beaks like pick-axes.

It was very cold, but peaceful. I wandered further, and found myself in an older, less well-tended corner of the cemetery, right up against the wall of the neighbouring convent. Ivy clung to the crumbling walls, and dead weeds sprouted in abundance, sometimes thrusting up through hard-packed patches of snow. There was no one else around. Lined up along the base of the wall was a jumbled collection of miscellaneous, very old, headstones—they'd been collected from different parts of the cemetery and lined up here while someone decided what to do with them. I bent down and got out my phrase book, determined to decipher some of the names. Who knows, I thought, there might be someone famous here, perhaps someone who has actually condescended to stay buried. It was hard work, but I'm pretty sure one of them was Mr Magoo.

Working my way along the wall I came to a low crumbling archway, leading to a kind of annex to the main cemetery. This part was really old; perhaps once it had been part of the original graveyard, within the convent's walls. It was completely overgrown with wild grasses and weeds—all dead after the winter's snows, like a Hammer Horror set. A shattered stone statue of an old soldier on a horse loomed in front of me. He had a broken sword and a fierce moustache. The horse was fat, and the old soldier was reigning it in, hard. The horse was sitting back on its haunches, the reigns biting into its mouth. Its eyes were wide and rolling. I stepped forward, wanting to get a better look at his face.

They were on the pedestal, right under the rear end of the horse. They'd been hidden by a pile of weeds. She saw me at the same instant I saw her. She was ashamed, I know she was, but she didn't show it. She waved me away, gesturing vigorously behind his head and silently mouthing 'piss off'. I didn't need any encouragement. I wasn't getting any pleasure from the sight. I stumbled back through the arch, slipping in the mud. It was disgusting, it was wrong. Something had happened. Sharon wasn't Sharon anymore.

'Steady on, mon ami, where are you going so fast?' I'd been staggering along without looking, and I'd not seen Jean-Paul. He held me out at arm's length, and for a second I thought he had a look of real concern on his face.

'Sharon . . .' I croaked.

'Sharon, mon ami? She will be back in a minute. She is just making love with Alexei. Through there.' Jean-Paul beamed. 'And next it will be the turn of Anton.' He clapped his companion on the back. Chekhov, who was standing nearby, smiled enthusiastically and rubbed his hands together. His fingernails were black, and there was earth clinging to his knuckles.

'We missed you at my grave,' he said, 'perhaps you would

like to see it now? It is not far from here.'

I've never known anyone to be so proud of six miserable feet of mud. 'No, no thank you,' I muttered.

After the graveyard antics were concluded, we went back to the hotel to freshen up. Some of us, no doubt, needed it more than others. I couldn't even bear to look at Sharon, let alone talk to her, and Sharon, once she'd figured the lie of the land, adopted the same policy towards me. There was an icy silence in the car. Even Alexei was subdued.

We stopped at Chekhov's place so he could pick up some things for later. It didn't look like much from the outside—an eighteenth-century façade on the Sadovaya Kolitso, with a plaque by the door. The place was a museum, of course, and there were quite a few tourists and visitors wandering around. Chekhov didn't seem to mind. He greeted them all with a cheery wave, answered a few questions, signed some autographs. At first he got in trouble with a babushka for stepping over the velvet ropes, but once he'd explained who he was, she was sweetness and light itself. Now there, I thought, goes a man with real influence.

In his bedroom, Chekhov sorted out some fresh underwear and a few other odds and ends. At least he still made an effort; Sartre was still in the suit he'd been buried in. Chekhov was different, surprisingly vain for a corpse. He made a huge fuss about sticking one of his ears back on with moustache wax. (I don't know what happened and I don't want to know, but when he and Sharon came back from the annex he had it tucked in his breast pocket.) He kept looking at himself in the mirror.

'But is it straight? Is it quite straight?'

We all had to gather round and assure him no one would ever guess it had ever been off in the first place.

Just before we left, Chekhov dashed across to the chest of

drawers. He took up a very handsome pair of solid silver hair brushes. He turned to Sharon.

'For you, my dear.'

Sharon thanked him and assured him they were beautiful. She kissed him on the cheek. She was making an extra fuss of everyone else, just to make me feel bad.

'Isn't he just the greatest?' she said, wrinkling her nose. 'And such a genius!' I could see Jean-Paul looking askance at this. Sexual jealousy may be a foible of the living alone, but intellectual pride reaches to the grave and beyond. Sharon, I must say, was never jealous of anybody for anything. She linked arms with the corpses and skipped downstairs, chattering away.

When we got to the hotel I went straight to my room. I lay on the chocolate bedspread and turned my face to the wall. My world was crumbling. I'd always thought that I understood Sharon, in a special way, a way no one else did. People used to say I was a fool, following her round like a faithful dog, never asking for anything in return. They used to say she was using me, but I'd never cared, before today. They didn't know her; I did. I knew her vulnerable moments, the moments when she'd turn to me with a question or a smile. Of course the lovers came and went—the stars, the producers, members of royalty, owners of supermarket chains, mounted policemen and swimming pool attendants. That had never bothered me, before, because I had something they didn't have, and never would have. I had a real friendship, with the real Sharon. I treasured that.

But that Sharon, the real Sharon, my Sharon—where had she gone? It was time to face facts. Ever since she'd taken up with Sartre, I'd known that I was losing her. She'd stopped looking at me in that special way. She'd stopped trusting me with her innermost fears and desires. Maybe she never had, maybe it had all been an act, specially tailored for my benefit, just like all the others. She was an actress after all. The years of fame, of adulation, of hob-nobbing with the rich and opinionated—maybe she wasn't immune, as I'd always thought. Certainly, she'd never seemed more strange to me. She was on a path to destruction, a path of her own choosing, and yet not of her own choosing. I picked up the phone. I had to give it one more shot. I had to, for Sharon's sake.

'Sharon? It's me. I want to see you.'

'Sure, Albert, come on up.' Her voice was cold.

'No. My place this time.'

She began to argue, but I cut through. 'Alone or not at all.'

There was a long pause, then the line went dead.

I got out my bag and began to pack. Whatever happened, I wasn't staying, I knew that much. When she knocked on the door I don't know if I was surprised or not. She stood just inside the doorway, her arms folded. She looked magnificent. Her brows were knitted and her nostrils flared. Her lips were pale. She was a warrior queen.

'Well?' she said.

'You told me to give it twenty-four hours. You said if I wanted to go home, you'd fly me personally. Well, I want to go home.'

The warrior queen vanished. She was just Sharon, looking tired. She came to sit beside me. 'We know each other too well for this.'

'Do we?'

She sighed. 'Okay, okay. Take the jet. I guess I'll see you in Paris.'

'Personally, Sharon. I want you to come with me.'

'Oh, man, if you think I'm flying out of here and missing the main event, you got another think coming. Why don't you wait until tomorrow? I'll come with you then.'

'You promised.'

'Oh for Chrissake be reasonable. Tomorrow. We'll go tomorrow.'

'Tomorrow will be too late. There is evil in this place. I fear for you.' Even as I said it, I realised just how true it was. I put a hand on her arm. She stood up quickly and when she turned her face was cold, the expression dead. 'You're talking about my friends.'

'I thought I was your friend.'

'So did I, Al. So did I.'

A dizzy gulf was opening in front of my feet, and Sharon was on the other side. 'Look, Sharon.' I was pleading now. 'I've got nothing against dead people, but it's just not healthy. Anton Chekhov's been dead since 1904. Think about it! That's more than forty years before the invention of television.'

'So?'

'You're alive. You need the living.'

'For your information Anton is a truly inspirational writer, and a wonderful, wonderful man. He sets my brain on fire.'

'And what about hygiene?'

'Godammit Albert, these are human beings you're talking about!'

'Dead human beings. Dead!'

'Alexei isn't dead.'

'No, but he's the devil incarnate.'

She was no longer looking at me with anger, but with scorn. 'You're just a bigot. I never realised.' Her green eyes blazed. 'Or, no . . .' she advanced on me, and stood looking down. 'That's not it at all. You're jealous.'

'Don't be ridiculous.'

'All these years, and you're jealous of some harmless fun. Well let me tell you, men like Anton and Jean-Paul, and Leo have done more for—'

'Leo? Who the hell's he?'

'Leo Tolstoy. He's a friend of Anton's, Anton asked him round for a drink.'

Something snapped. 'Oh my God!' I screamed at her.

'There's no end to it. Forget Alexei, but as for the others, for God's sake, show some respect! If not for yourself, for them! It's humiliating, it's degrading. It's disgusting! It's . . . it's . . . *necrophilia*!'

There. I'd said it. Sharon turned on her heel and walked out, slamming the door.

I felt numb, drained of all emotion. I sat on the bed for a minute to gather my wits. Suddenly this tiny room was overpoweringly stuffy, claustrophobic.

I was walking. Just walking. The cold snap was really starting to bite. My shoes were too thin and already I could feel the cold striking up through the soles. There were flurries of snow, and the pavement was slick with ice. The sun was low in the sky. It was already getting dark. I trudged on, not caring where I was going. I found myself crossing Red Square. St Basil's was lit up with a huge neon statue of the Virgin Mary, erected as a public service by the VneshEconomBank of the CIS.

Strangely, there was a ruddy glow over the western skyline. I thought I heard a dull boom. I was thinking about Sharon. All the fight had gone out of me and I missed her terribly already. Maybe she was right. Maybe I was just jealous. It was all too sad for words.

To my right was G.U.M., the department store. Calvin Klein, Dior. Neon and plate glass. The cobbles under my feet were old, old, old. And cold, cold, cold. On my left, the red brick walls of the Kremlin paraded slowly by. Crouching in their shadow was the squat low structure of Lenin's Tomb. There were a lot of people about, shuffling along fast, with their heads down. No one spoke and the only sound was the shuffling of many feet, muffled by the falling snow. They were all headed the same way; east, away from the glow in the sky. I bumped into a woman with a large parcel under her arm. The parcel went flying and I scrambled to pick it up. Looking up into her face I saw her lips were blue and her eyes were glassy.

'Ogromnaya spassibo,' she said. Thank you very much. She took the parcel and, when her fingers brushed mine, they were cold. I wanted to ask her about the glow in the sky, but she was gone, lost in the crowd. I carried on across the square, heading for Lenin's Tomb. I seemed to be the only one walking that way—crowds of people streamed past me, all with their heads down, many of them clutching parcels. They parted to let me through, like a river round a rock.

There was another boom—this time unmistakable—and the glow in the west became brighter. I thought I heard a distant roar, like a football crowd. The people around me hurried all the more. There was something going on. I stopped a small hurrying figure. It was a girl, only about twelve. She had a huge fleshy mole in the middle of her forehead.

'What is it?' I asked. I pointed at the glow.

'Frantsusi,' she said. The French. She ducked past me and away.

To my left were a group of men. They were building a barricade out of old horses. They spoke soothingly to the shivering animals, coaxing them to lie down, one on top of the other.

'Shouldn't those be dead?' I called out, but they didn't understand.

'Frantsusi,' they said, and pointed at the glow in the sky. There was yet another boom, still harsher, louder, and a red streak of light shot into the sky—a rocket or a shell. The men went back to their work. A parachute flare began to descend, casting a green glow across their faces.

I slipped on an uneven cobble and almost went down. I realised I'd seriously misjudged the weather. I was shivering uncontrollably, and my feet were numb. I could feel the hairs in my nostrils crackle as they froze solid. My feet were unwieldy blocks of stone, useless, heavy. I realised if I didn't get warm I was going to freeze. In front of me now was the old Lenin museum, grim and forbidding. G.U.M., with its familiar plate glass, clothing displays, electronic tills and price tags, beckoned to my right, so I turned in that direction.

Then the snow really came down. It flew in my face like a plague of moths. G.U.M. vanished. The wind howled across the ancient cobbles, picking up the fallen snow and flinging it with renewed fury. Lenin's museum vanished. There was no sign of St Basil's. I was alone in a white-out so complete I might have been inside a huge ping pong ball. Hunched over, shielding my eyes, I staggered blindly forward, slipping and stumbling. People were still streaming past, looming suddenly at me out of the snow. They were running now, all of them, parcels in their hands, some barefoot, some of them in ragged clothes. They were moving faster, and faster, and as I struggled to cut across the tide, they swerved to avoid me, jumping nimbly aside like rabbits, parcels clutched to their chests. Every once in a while I glimpsed another face: bloodless lips and frightened, apologetic stares. A squat, low, blockhouse structure rose out of the gloom ahead. I staggered towards it.

'Hey,' I shouted, 'open up. It's cold out here. I'm going to freeze, for Chrissake!' I hammered on the huge brass doors, but there was no reply. 'Let me in!' I screamed. The cold was working its way up my legs. I couldn't feel my lips. Where are your friends when you need them? My fingers were numb. I fell to my knees.

I was dreaming about flying cathedrals.

'Alberchik?'

I'm dreaming.

'Al?'

I'm still dreaming.

'Mon ami?'

Someone is massaging my hands.

Light.

My head is captured by the pincers of a great stag beetle, a beetle without compassion.

A beetle without compassion is like a head without a hole.

Where is my lobster?

Jean-Paul Sartre keeps his cigarettes in a hole in his head.

The cathedral is flying, buttresses and all.

I was lying in the dark. There was a stone staircase in front of me, going down. Lamp brackets threw cold pools of light onto the smooth stone walls. It wasn't cold anymore. I got to my feet and looked behind me. Two huge copper doors, shut fast. I went down. The stairs turned a corner, went along for a distance, then doubled back and turned again. By now I had no idea where I was in relation to the surface. Eventually I turned another corner and came out in a central chamber. In the middle of the chamber was a glass-topped coffin mounted on a stone plinth.

The coffin was empty. Lenin was sitting on top of the plinth, swinging his stumpy legs and drumming his heels against the stone. He was humming a peasant folk-song, but I didn't know the tune. He was bright yellow, the yellow of crayons. His goatee beard also appeared to have been crayoned, a deep chocolate brown. There was an overpowering smell of formaldehyde. He hadn't seen me, so I coughed. He jumped a mile.

'In the name of all that's holy don't sneak up on a man like that! What do you want?'

'Nothing. I was cold.'

'How did you get in?'

'I don't know.'

He shrugged. 'In that case, come in.'

'The French are coming,' I said.

He shrugged. 'They come and go. French, Germans, Americans, it makes no difference.'

'Can't you do something?'

He drew himself up and stared at me sternly. 'Look at the floor!'

I looked at the floor. There was a groove worn in the stone.

'For sixty years they came, shuffling by. Rain or shine for sixty years. I made my difference. Make your own difference.'

'But it's all fucked up now. It's been fucked for years.'

'It was fucked from the start.'

'Can you at least give me some directions?'

He sighed. 'Come on, I'll show you the nearest Metro.'

We went up the steps and outside. I braced myself for the cold, but I didn't feel it at all. The night was dark, and the snow was falling harder than ever. The wind had dropped and it fell like curtains, now, straight down. Inches deep, it was drifted in doorways, against walls, against the tyres of cars. It dusted my head and shoulders and clung to my eyelashes. It was so cold now the snow was dry: it crunched under my shoes like sand at the beach.

I followed Lenin across the deserted square. There was a clop clop sound behind us, and a troop of horsemen galloped past, swords drawn, the hooves of the horses striking sparks on the cobbles. They were in bright red tunics and they wore tall shakos with death's-head emblems. I caught a glimpse of a childish face and a bristling moustache, then they were gone. There was an ear-splitting explosion, and I ducked. The glow was closer now, and it was clearly the glow of a huge fire. The ruddy light flickered and jumped on the rooftops. A shell screamed overhead.

We passed a group of teenagers struggling to lever cobblestones out of the ground. They were drinking and singing.

A squad of soldiers in bandoliers and greatcoats ran towards us, their heads hunched down under steel helmets.

'Nemtsi!' they shouted as they came. A tank rumbled into the square, its turret swivelling like a blind man's head. I looked about: Lenin had vanished. I was about to shout a warning to the teenagers, when a horse came charging out of a side street. It was the Marlboro Man, on a white charger. His checked shirt was crisp and clean. He drew up next to the teenagers and shot them, carefully, one after the other, with his six gun. Then he stood up in his stirrups. A woman began to scream from an alleyway, and an eviscerated dog fell from a sixth storey window.

'Yippeeee!' shouted the Marlboro Man. He looked around and his horse reared up and neighed. The tank lumbered past and down the street he'd just come up. He walked his horse over to me. 'Say, pardner, where's the party?' He drew his pistol and took aim.

There was a tug at my elbow. I looked down: it was the lobster.

'This way.' It ducked into a doorway and I followed, just as the shot rang out. On the wall beside me I saw a sign: Metro.

The lobster jumped up and clung to my neck as we joined a river of bodies, flowing fast through a double set of aluminium framed doors. They were all dead. They poured down the escalators and carried us with them. Their faces were set, their lips blue, their eyes dull, smeared and dry.

There was no question of choosing a direction of travel. We were carried along, down platforms and along empty black tunnels, up ornately carved stairways, past friezes and bas-reliefs, over humpback bridges, down winding corridors. Strange sights floated past: beggars hunched in alcoves along the way, hawkers peddling pornographic leaflets, starving children and peasant families with no feet in their shoes. My face was pressed into a rough hairy overcoat.

I began to dream.

'Wake up.' The lobster was standing over me. It was very

warm. I sat up and looked around. We were in a familiar green corridor, and beside me was a set of lift doors. I pressed the button for the thirteenth floor.

Sharon was lying on the couch, with her hands behind her head, smoking a cigarette. Alexei was sitting at her feet. Sharon was talking. 'It was my idea, not Paul's. I don't think he would have suggested it. But I really wanted to bring something to that scene, I wanted to shock them, you know? And it was true for the character, so . . . I had them in my hand, and I just thought what the hell, and I just walked out, left them in the trailer. I didn't say anything. Then after the first take Paul took me aside, kinda blushing but kinda excited, and he said, "You sure about this?" I said, "Yes, Paul, I'm sure . . ." and so that was how it happened.'

'What do you want?' said Alexei, irritably.

Sharon caught sight of me in the doorway. 'Albert, for Chrissake, you had me really worried. Where the hell have you been?' The expression on her face changed, and she stared at me more closely. I knew then that something was wrong.

'What? What is it?' I said.

She didn't reply but came towards me. I glanced at Jean-Paul and Chekhov, who were sitting down, passing a bottle. They seemed to have made friends again. There was an old, white-bearded man in high boots and a peasant smock sitting between them, taking his turn with the bottle. He had the bushiest eyebrows I've ever seen. When they noticed me, they did a double take, looked at one another, and grinned. Jean-Paul held out the bottle.

'You better have some of this, mon ami.'

Oh no, I thought. It can't be.

Very gently, Sharon took my wrist. I realised she was checking my pulse. What a fool I'd been, going out in weather like that.

Alexei jumped up. 'Time to go.' He strode out.

I caught him up in reception. 'Alexei,' I said, 'I'm leaving. I want to check out.'

Alexei laughed and waved me away. 'Check out any time you like.'

'Just come to the party,' said Sharon, 'then I'll fly you home.' She adjusted my collar.

The Idiot was vast, an aircraft hangar done in marble and polished granite. Pillars to the roof, plaster cherubim and seraphim, pilasters around the walls, gilt mirrors, caryatids—the works. There was a huge dance floor and a band. They were playing Eagles medleys. There were hundreds of tables arranged round the floor, with white starched cloths and silver cutlery. The place was packed and clouds of cigarette smoke hung so thick it looked like the battle of Borodino. The women were all in evening gowns and the men were in tails and bow-ties—except for the ones in uniform.

Everyone was there. I recognised Magic Johnson and the Dalai Lama straight off, as they sauntered over with Gérard to say hello. I watched very closely, but Sharon didn't look into the Dalai's face, not once. Looking around, I spotted a white ten-gallon hat sticking up above the heads on the far side of the room. Jack Nicholson was leaning on a pilaster to one side, in dark glasses and a paisley shirt. Surprisingly, even Michael Douglas had managed to get himself invited. He was talking to Jack.

They put us at a table in the centre, next to the dance floor, with Alexei, the dead, and a lot of people I didn't know.

'Here, Albert.' Sharon patted the chair next to her. Ever since my demise, Sharon had been kindness and consideration itself. On the way over, she'd told Alexei I didn't have to drive any more, and put me next to her in the back of the limo. She put her hand on my knee as we drove, and kept reaching up to stroke my hair.

Now, she fussed over me and settled me in my chair. Her hand went back to my thigh and she leaned over to adjust my collar. 'Poor baby,' she whispered in my ear. Hidden by the tablecloth, her hand inched a little higher.

The truth is, it did nothing for me. Nothing at all. It might as well have been happening to someone else. I realised what a terrible drag it was going to be, being dead. I couldn't taste. I couldn't feel anything. Sound was muffled, like being underwater. Vision was smeary, like a pair of slept-in contact lenses. I could have kicked myself. A moment's thoughtlessness, and here I was. Mortified. It seemed so random, so pointless, and yet so irreversible. I checked in one of the gilt mirrors, hoping against hope it would turn out to be just a bad case of hypothermia, but no such luck. It was unmistakable—that bluish tinge around the lips, the glassy eyes. What a fool I'd been.

'Ce n'est pas drôle, hein?' Sartre whispered hoarsely in my ear. I caught the malicious pleasure in his eye. I couldn't blame him. I'd treated him badly, I knew. 'Don't worry, mon vieux,' he continued, 'it gets worse.'

The only pleasure was to be derived from the glowering looks I was getting from Alexei, across the table. It's a sad fact that delight in the discomfort of our detractors dies hard. Very hard. I grinned maliciously, and gave him a mock salute.

The waiter came round. Jean-Paul tried to order vodka and found they sold it by the gram, not the bottle. He ordered six kilos each for himself, Leo and Anton. Even the waiter was impressed. Jean-Paul looked enquiringly at me. 'Same for you, mon vieux?'

'Thanks, I don't feel like drinking. Maybe after dinner.' All three of the dead nudged one another and exchanged glances. The old man was smirking into his beard, and I took a strong dislike to him.

I turned back to the waiter. Alexei was in the process of ordering caviar followed by sturgeon. Sharon got out her salad bag. I was interested in the fish. Through Jean-Paul, who translated in between fits of the giggles, I asked if it was fresh.

'Yes.' said the waiter. 'Fresh.'

'Not frozen?'

'Freshly frozen.'

'What do you mean? It's either frozen, or it's fresh.'

The waiter looked at me haughtily. 'Monsieur,' he said, 'it's at least as fresh as you.'

Across the table, Tolstoy was stuffing his own beard into his mouth to muffle his laughter. I abandoned the idea of fish and went for something called Chicken Tabac. How far wrong can you go with chicken? Chekhov offered me his vodka bottle. 'Seriously,' he said, 'you'd better drink up. Prevents decay.' I hesitated. Perhaps he was right. The last thing I needed was my ears falling off. 'Trust me,' he said, 'I'm a doctor.' They all hooted and fell about at this, but I took the bottle, just to be on the safe side. The vodka went down like water.

When the meal arrived, Chicken Tabac turned out to be a half chicken which looked as if it had been hit with a sledge-hammer, then fried in garlic. In fact that's exactly what had happened to it. I hadn't eaten for hours, but when I saw the dish in front of me I realised that eating was indeed a thing of the past. I simply had no appetite, none at all. It wasn't that I was revolted or disgusted by it. It was simply that the prospect of shredding dead flesh with my teeth no longer held any meaning or relevance for me. It struck me simply as an absurd, onerous chore. I cut a few pieces for the sake of my dignity, but there was no concealing my lack of enthusiasm from the delighted dead, who were watching me like kites.

'Go on, Albert, get it down you.'

'What's the matter, mon ami? Not hungry?'

I called the waiter: 'Six kilos of Stolichnaya please.'

The corpses howled with delight, and money changed hands.

'Cheer up, mon vieux,' said Sartre. 'One is still what one is going to cease to be, and already what one is going to become. One lives one's death, one dies one's life.'

'Thanks,' I said, 'that's a big help.'

Chekhov grinned. 'Let him alone. He's in mourning for his life.'

Tolstoy cleared his throat. 'When I was fifty years old, I asked myself and all the learned men around me what I am and what is the meaning of life, and received the answer that I am a fortuitous concatenation of atoms and that life has no meaning but is itself an evil.' He looked around him pugnaciously, and emptied his bottle. Now, I hated him.

Sharon moved her hand a little higher on my thigh. 'I'm sorry about this afternoon,' she said.

'So am I.' I felt nothing. Nothing. I caught Sartre watching me keenly. He winked.

Chekhov, Tolstoy and Sartre were talking about women, passing the bottle around. Tolstoy was (inordinately) interested in Sartre's ideas about sexual freedom, but Chekhov thought he was just kidding himself. 'You're running counter to human nature, Jean-Paul.'

'There is no such thing as human nature.'

'Just because we don't understand it doesn't mean it doesn't exist.'

'It's not a question of human nature,' thundered Tolstoy, 'women must learn to know their place.'

Sartre turned to Chekhov. 'To an existentialist the idea of human nature is merely bad faith.' Chekhov laughed indulgently.

'Faith is the only possible foundation of existence,' said Tolstoy.

'Existence has no possible foundation,' said Jean-Paul.

'I once knew a woman,' said Chekhov, 'a most extraordinary creature, an actress at the Maly Theatre, such a delicate weak little neck, a most delectable . . .'

'Women!' I shouted, getting to my feet. 'I'll tell you about women!' Chekhov paused, a sardonic smile on his lips. Everyone stopped and listened. But I had nothing to say. There was only one woman I'd ever cared about in my life, and now I was dead. 'Women,' I said. 'Women are . . . *women* are . . . alive.' I sat down and picked up the nearest vodka bottle.

Chekhov went back to his story.

By now most people had finished eating. The band was playing 'Hotel California'. People flooded the dance floor; huge ungainly men and women rotated without reserve, mixing with young and old alike. Chekhov and Jean-Paul were arguing again—something about social action and the revolution. Jean-Paul was throwing words like bourgeois around, but Chekhov didn't seem to understand that he was being insulted. He laughed.

'But surely no one takes that stuff seriously still?'

Angry, Sartre retorted that he didn't understand how such a sensitive writer of tragedy could be so insensitive to political life. Chekhov slammed his fist on the table. 'I do not write tragedy!' he screamed. 'I write comedy! COMEDY!'

'C'mon, Albert,' said Sharon, 'let's you and me cut the rug.'

The thing about being dead is you don't feel like doing anything, but you don't feel like not doing anything either. We danced, my Sharon and I—I felt nothing. Sharon held me close—nothing. She moved in closer and closer—still nothing. Michael Douglas . . . Nothing nothing nothing.

'Oh dear,' she said. A clump of my hair had come out in her fingers. She smoothed it back with a lick of spit. I didn't care. I watched the other dancers. Warm people pressing up against other warm people. Sharon leaned close and whispered in my ear. It was like listening to someone at the end of a cardboard tube.

'Albert,' she said, 'I've only ever really wanted to be with you, you know that, don't you?'

'That's nice.' I was aware of her hand, moving on my thigh. I grinned at her, glassily.

Alexei stood up and shouted. 'SILENCE.'

The dance continued and the band played on.

Alexei pulled a Colt forty-fife out of his pocket and emptied it into the ceiling.

Silence fell, and the dancers resumed their seats, Sharon and I among them.

Alexei cleared his throat, and tucked his thumbs into his fob pockets. 'Ladies and Gentlemen. Boys and Girls. Welcome.'

There was a roar of approval.

'I will now make to you speech about government of Russia, about future of economy, and about projections of economic success in financial and industrial sectors of our great country.' Murmurs of disapproval. Alexei raised his glass and looked around him.

'I say to you this—BUY RUSSIAN!'

Tumultuous applause.

'You're talking about a benign dictatorship?' This was Jean-Paul of course.

'Shut up.'

'What the hell,' said Sharon, 'it's worth a shot.'

Jean-Paul sighed.

Alexei leapt onto the table. With a great crash, he swept cutlery, uneaten food and crockery to the floor with a booted foot. From there he addressed the whole restaurant. 'My friends,' he said, 'I am simple man. What I do, I do for Russia, for Motherland.' He looked down, as if suddenly taken shy. He toyed with the toe of his boot. 'Many of you here tonight,' he continued, 'have travelled far. You have come because tonight is special occasion. We have with us here, tonight, very special guest . . .' here Sharon nudged me with anticipation, but I was only half aware. My attention had been caught by a tiny tapping sound. Tip-tap, it went, tip-tap tippity-tip. I could barely hear it in my deadened state, but something told me it was important. I looked around blearily, trying to locate the source of the sound. Alexei rumbled on. 'A guest whose delicacy, whose charm, whose exquisite sensibility in all fields of endeavour is known to all here tonight.'

Tip-tap, tip tip tip. There it came again. I hunted the room with my eyes and finally I saw it. It was the lobster. It was outside, in the snow and the cold of the darkened street, tapping on the window with one its feelers. It wanted to be let in. I glanced back at Sharon. She was listening to the speech.

'But first, dear friends, let me present to you the incomparable, the one and only,'—pausing to build the suspense—'Miss SHERRYN STONE!' There was a burst of wild applause. The crowd cheered and surged forward, men, women, children. On one side of the room a fight broke out and chairs flew in the air. Someone else was hit in the face by a flying sturgeon.

The Marlboro Man stepped out of the crowd, twirling his whip. 'Now now, folks, one at a time please, one at a time, give the lady some room, step right up, that's right . . .' Sharon jumped up onto the table and began to gesture for silence as the table rose swiftly and silently on hydraulic legs. Gradually the crowd settled and she began her speech.

I had been pushed to the back by the rush. Seeing my chance, I slipped under a nearby table, and began to crawl in what I thought was the direction of the windows. It was a long way to travel. The starched linen tablecloths hung nearly to the floor, and it was dim and peaceful down there. I was crawling along a faintly glowing white corridor, the floor littered with chicken bones, empty bottles and feet.

Sharon's speech continued: 'Dear dear friends, one and

all, I can't tell you, I simply can't tell you what it means to be among you on this most special of all specially special occasions . . .' Wild applause. I continued, changing direction from time to time, working my way towards the windows. '. . . dear friends . . . Let's take a moment to think about what I've just said. Friends. It's not often in our lives that we can say that word, and really mean it, I mean really mean it. I mean, really . . .'

I crawled out from under a table by slipping between the velvet-clad thighs of a sort of impresario, or possibly a mountebank, who sat sprawled in his chair with his top hat pushed back on his sweaty forehead and a broad grin on his shiny red face. He was gazing, like everyone else, with rapt attention at Sharon. '. . . so when I say a friend, I really really mean it, in the truly true sense of the real word . . .'

I was at the window. I knelt on the floor and pressed my cold forehead against the cold glass. There he was on the other side of the pane, standing in the snowy street, his dear little carapace white with frost. He was signalling to me, tapping on the window pane with his feelers: short short short . . . long, long, long . . . short short short . . . long, long, long. No other sound penetrated the glass, but behind the lobster occasional flashes of brilliant orange light revealed a nightmare world of crumbling masonry and flying debris.

Behind the lobster a crowd was gathering. Women and children in ragged clothes, men on crutches with bandaged heads. The halt and the lame, the lame and the halt. They were crowding forward out of the alleys, out of the Metro stations, hesitantly, shyly, from all the dark corners of the world, or so it seemed, clutching their bundles done up with string. Their faces were pale and pinched, their eyes were huge and beseeching. Many bore terrible suppurating wounds. The women held up their babies and the men held up their children.

I wished it wasn't so, but I could barely feel. I could neither cry nor weep, feel neither horror nor despair. I was dead. My heart had turned to stone. But the lobster smiled and pointed. I looked to where the lobster was pointing. He was pointing to the huge double doors, which opened onto the street. I headed for the doors, and the people outside kept pace, moving from window to window. Behind me, in the lighted room, the gathering of friends were still as statues, drinking Sharon's every word.

'. . . modest doesn't even begin to describe this guy—let me tell you, I had myself one hell of a job just persuading him to be here at all tonight . . .'—a ripple of appreciative laughter—'. . . in fact, the only way I could get him here—was to pretend it was my party and not his at all!' Shouts of delighted laughter rang from the roof. 'And so I know, dear, dear friends, that you'll all join with me now in welcoming our nearest, our dearest, our oldest and most beloved friend of all—ladies and gentlemen, I give you the guest of honour, the soft centre of all our hearts—ladies and gentlemen, let's put it together for the one and only—*Albert! C'mon, Al, get yourself up here!*'

I was still several yards from the door. I spun around to face the room, as the band struck up a heavy metal rendition of 'Happy Birthday' and the crowd roared and applauded like mad. Sharon was looking around her as she realised for the first time I wasn't behind her. There was a moment's confusion, some scattered laughter, and an embarrassed hush. Sharon shaded her eyes and searched the crowd. 'Al? Are you out there? C'mon, don't be shy . . .'

People were beginning to look around. The impresario's gaze was swivelling in my direction. I had seconds in which to act. I turned back towards the door.

'Zer he iss!' warbled the impresario in a cheerfully strangulated tenor. I decided he was probably a mountebank after all. On all sides they took up the cry: 'Zer! Zer! Zer he issss!' All eyes were on me. It was appalling. I managed a glassy grin.

'Albert!' called Sharon from across the room. 'It's all for you, babe, it's all for you.'

'Ladies and gentlemen,' I began. 'It's . . . a real . . . really . . .' My gaze roved desperately. All I could see was a sea of smiling faces. Teeth. Glazed eyes.

I was only yards from the door. I raised my arm, as if to show there was nothing up my sleeve—and sprang for the doors, with my awkward knock-kneed gait, my shoes catching in the shag pile, forcing my corpse forward at breakneck pace. My intentions became plain to the crowd. There was a gasp of horror, and then from the other side of the room, another cry: '*Stop him!*' They took it up. 'Stop him! Stop him!' There was a howl behind me, and a ring of drawn steel, as the mountebank flung himself after me. But he was too late. My lifeless fingers closed on the ornate brass door handle. I pulled the doors wide.

A flurry of snow burst in on a gust of cold clean air—and with it a cacophony of sound. Machine guns, distant but menacing, chattered in the night. The terrifying whine of a nebelwerfer started up, only a few blocks away. Voices, sirens, shouts of fear and anger, wails and moans, the crying of babies, demented laughter, the tramping of feet. The dull boom of a shell exploding in the distance. The sharp crack of rifle fire. The throbbing drone of many aircraft.

They were there, the lobster at their head. They raised their hands in supplication, and they flooded into the room. The diners backed away with a collective moan of terror. More and more of them crowded forward, out of the shadows, pushing forward towards the tables. They came perhaps halfway across the floor, and then the diners stopped retreating. They took up their steely dinner knives. A sudden, terrible, silence fell. It was Jean-Paul who broke it.

'VIVE LA RÉVOLUTION!' he screamed.

The diners screamed, the dead screamed, everyone

screamed, and battle was joined. A shell burst in the street outside, shattering the windows; diners and dead alike were cut to ribbons by shards of flying glass. Plaster fell from the roof as another shell landed, and bodies were tossed through the air like dolls. I saw Sharon, bestriding her table like a rock in a stormy sea, the light of battle in her eyes, laying about her to left and right. There was blood streaming down her temples, and her dress was off one shoulder. She was waving a huge imperial flag.

'*Liberté!*' she screamed. '*Égalité! Fraternité!*' She was magnificent, if doomed. 'Goodbye, Sharon,' I whispered from the door.

The doors were still open. I staggered out into the night. Coming out of a side street I found myself standing again on the old, cold cobbles of Red Square. I wasn't far from Lenin's Tomb, and I started towards it. As I arrived at the great brass doors, I looked back and saw another massive explosion: Saint Basil's disappeared in a vast blossom of orange and red flame. The whole cathedral, buttresses and all. Masonry and metal clattered about me. A rocket shot into the sky with a great woosh. The city was falling. The sky was falling. Jets screamed overhead. Everything was fucked. There was a sudden concussion and I staggered forward. Feeling the back of my head, I found a piece of brick buried in my skull. I used it to wedge the great brass doors shut behind me.

The chamber was empty. It was quiet here. I climbed onto the plinth and eased open the glass-lidded coffin. I climbed in, lay down on the cold smooth satin and lowered the lid. I lay still, my hands across my breast, my unblinking eyes fixed on nothing. I vowed to myself, and to all creation, never to move again.